THE HOUSES OF ALPHONSO

By the same author

Novel
The Coral Rooms

Poetry
Watercourse
The Long Gap
Wings of A Stranger

Anthology
Crossing Water: Contemporary Poetry of the English-Speaking Caribbean, Editor.

Acknowledgements
I wish to thank Malaika Favorite, Maxine McClean, Dr. Eronini Egbujor, and Dr. Ray Chandrasekara for their always engaging and provocative critical insights; and to acknowledge Dr. Hilary Beckles's fine book, *Corporate Power in Barbados*, for its inspiration.
A.K

THE HOUSES OF ALPHONSO

ANTHONY KELLMAN

PEEPAL TREE

First published in Great Britain in 2004
Peepal Tree Press
17 King's Avenue
Leeds LS6 1QS
England

ISBN 1 900715 82 1

Cover painting: Aziza McMillan, *The Little Chattel Houses*
Cover photograph: Malaika Favorite

Peepal Tree gratefully acknowledges Arts Council support

PART ONE

CHAPTER ONE

'Alphonso? You're very quiet up there! What's the matter?' Simone's voice startled me. I was meant to be packing, but I'd just found *The Volcanoes of Sao Paulo*. I'd had the book since high school, had brought it with me to the States. It was a keepsake, a memento of my devious youth. At the top of page eight, I read the inscription in my handwriting: Harold Alphonso Hutson. Form 4B. Combermere School. My mother had gotten it from the Simpsons, the white family for whom she worked as a maid. I'd never shown Simone the book that contained so many clues to my restlessness, and her voice, stealing upstairs unannounced, threatened a violation of my privacy. The clues within the book had made the buried pages of my past flutter and turn more decisively inside me. I felt impelled to act in a way I had never done before. But it would have to be on my own. I placed the book with its eviscerated pages back into the packing carton.

'I'm fine! ...Simone, I'm not going to move again!' I heard myself shout with inexplicable certainty. An uncanny silence enveloped the house.

'What did you say?' I turned around to see Simone advancing up the staircase. As her upper body came fully into view, I got up from my squatting position and moved toward her. I felt drained and rested my left hand on the railing for support. It was as if I had relived my entire life in just a matter of minutes. I sat down on the third step from the top and stretched my feet out to rest on the fourth and fifth steps respectively. She was standing right before me now, her eyes wide with rage.

'Don't play with me, Alphonso. Don't play with my mind nor the children's.' She had folded her arms. 'If you ain't moving to Savannah, what you plan to do? Cancel the lease on your apartment? You'd lose your deposit. I tell you one thing: you're not staying here.'

I realized Simone thought I was trying to manipulate her, trying to get her back under the pretence of not moving again. This time, though, she had misread my intentions.

She repeated, 'You're not staying here, Alphonso.'

'I'm not,' I said. 'I'm going to Barbados.'

Simone's face turned pensive. 'You *are* serious,' she said. She had long urged me to do just this.

'You got that right. Remember Aunt Lolita and my parents' house there? Well, it's time I go and see 'bout that. I could use a holiday, anyhow.'

'A holiday? What you going to do about work – and all this ... ' she motioned to the cartons.

'It'll be fine. I'm due some time off. I'll tell them I've got some urgent family business. I'll arrange to get this stuff picked up when I get back.'

Simone rolled her eyes, but then said, 'You should've gone months ago. When she sent you the keys.' She rested her right hand on my shoulder. 'I really hope this will change things for you. I really hope so.'

'Thanks,' I said. 'Who knows, I may even buy some more property there. A retirement home on the coast, perhaps. If I do, Martin'll finally get some sleep, you don't think?'

Martin was my best friend, drinking and pool partner. As a real American (and a real estate agent) he thoroughly disapproved of my reluctance to invest in property. But behind my levity, something fluttered like dogwood leaves shaken by a gusty wind. I knew the challenge that awaited me in Barbados, the ghostly confrontations that were real and necessary.

This was the eighth time in ten years that I'd packed some of my worldly goods in the cartons that nested in the room like islands. The musky smell of cardboard always filled me with a sense of newness but also with a sense of things ended. It was an odor I had become all too familiar with over the years. After some sixteen years in the United States, after so much movement and exploration, I could no longer convince myself that the habit of frequent moving was ordinary and natural. The truth was my inner turmoil far exceeded the outer activity. But not even Simone knew the extent of my inner journeys, my inner wrestling with my past. These I kept bottled.

★   ★   ★

It was four months ago when I first told Simone of my planned transfer to Savannah. If she'd gone along with me, it would have been her eighth acquiescence in ten years of marriage. When I made the disclosure, the look on her face indicated that she was vacillating, as if an inner hand was holding her back and an inner voice warning that if she went along with me this time, it would be as good as signing a death warrant on her and the children. I knew that in the past she'd gone along with me because she believed that children should be raised in a complete family unit where they would receive the immediate nurturing of both parents. She'd hoped and prayed that I would change. So I wasn't surprised to sense the struggle going on inside her

She'd grown tired of hoping, year after year, for a change in me that never came. Lucinda, who had just started elementary school in Louisiana when we moved to Florence, and who'd had to change schools again when we

9

moved to Martinez a year later, was undoubtedly having problems of adjustment.

Simone looked steadily at me that late afternoon, three weeks before the Easter holiday weekend. We sat in the sun room to the left front of the house where she could keep an eye on the girls playing in the front yard. The pink and white azalea bushes were in bloom.

I knew that she loved this nine-roomed two-storey house which we had rented for the past year. The oak panels and base boards suggested it could have been built in the early 1920s. Ten-foot high ceilings. Arched front porch with Romanesque columns. Ancient club foot tub in the main bathroom. There was an ultramodern bathroom too, and outside, vacant lots at the sides of the house created a sense of privacy for her when she watered or mulched or pruned the azalea bushes.

Simone said, 'If you leave this time, we're not going with you.'

'What you said?' I asked. 'You make the decisions in this house now?'

'I'm staying here with the kids. You can keep on running as long as you want to, but count us out.'

Her meaning was clear, but I rolled my eyes and shook my head, not taking her seriously. The phone rang, so I went to answer it. I shouted to Simone that her mother was on the line, and I went to the bathroom. As I came out, I heard Simone say, 'It was the hardest thing I ever done in my life, giving him such an ultimatum...' Eavesdropping was not my usual style, but I stayed at the top of the stairs. Simone was out of sight in the 'lazy-boy', but I could hear clearly.

'...But now it's done, Mama, I gotta say I feel a satisfying sense of release.' Simone's voice did indeed sound liberated, filled with anticipation. I suspected that, in the past, she'd discussed our marriage problems with her mother, and I knew her mother had never been very fond of me. Yet, deep down I still hoped that her mother wouldn't influence Simone against me.

'Oh, it's so good to hear you, Mama,' I heard her say. 'A breath of fresh air... I love you too.' Then, to my surprise, I heard what sounded like sobs, deep raking sobs. Several minutes passed and Simone said, 'I'm all right, Mama... I know he loves me, but I think he's taking out his frustrations on me. It just isn't fair. For years I just felt driven into the ground. The children. I stuck it out for the children...'

'....No, Mama, they're not doing as well as they should do because of all the moving. That's where I drew the line. Lucinda was the first to pout and throw tantrums. Denise soon followed. Something had to give. I'd reached my saturation point. But even though I cussed and threatened to leave him, he still wouldn't change. In fact, things just got worse...

'Yes, Mama, I know I've got to let him go. He knows if he moves to Savannah, he's going alone... Why I put up with it so long? Like I said, the kids. And also I love him. I hoped he'd change... How's Dad doin'? How's his prostate... It may not be a good idea for you to come up at this time, Mama. I'll visit you. We'd have fewer distractions that way. And I'd love to see Dad. Is that good?'

I heard Simone laugh as I closed the bathroom door and went under the shower that ran like the strings on an out-of-tune guitar. The quality of my guilt plucked at my insides. She loved me. I loved her. I meant her no harm.

Dinner was awkward.

'In Savannah, we'll be able to go to the beach more often,' I said hopefully. I looked from her to the children and back again. She said nothing. She had joined the children in a conspiracy of silence, although their silences were differently motivated. Only their mouths masticating the tuna casserole could be heard, smacking like castanets.

'Me and the girls,' Simone said, her eyes locked into mine. 'We ain't moving with you.' Her words floated out effortlessly, glided forward and upward, and calmly possessed the house like a familiar. They hung like Spanish moss from my ear lobes (I kept pulling at my ears to get rid of them), from the chandeliers above the dining table, from the frames of paintings, from the oak-stained arch separating the dining room from the den. They hung, and they softly echoed. Even though I'd heard and overheard her intentions earlier, my mouth dropped open. The shock was new because her words had been delivered with the whole family there. Suddenly, they seemed larger, harsher, more horrible than on the phone. I wouldn't lose my girls!

'Excuse me?' I said. My mouth dropped open again.

Before I could close it and take fresh breath, Simone said, 'Not now, Alphonso. We'll discuss this later.' As always, she was concerned for the kids, protecting them. She smiled as they reached over to scoop slices of mocha cheesecake on to their plates. Her darlings, she called them. Her smile was an open field which contained them both.

I stared at her. For the rest of the meal, I just stared at her.

'You can't mean what you said, right?' I began, leaning in the doorway of our bedroom. (I had been banished to the upstairs guest room.) 'Come August, we're outta here, you know.'

'I sound like I was joking?' Simone turned on the bed towards the sound of my voice and put down the *Essence* she was reading.

'No. You didn't *sound* like you were joking. But you were joking, weren't you?'

'No, I wasn't.'

I stood in the doorway, gaping in disbelief. I was stunned that she hadn't buckled by now and changed her mind. I stared at her and at the ravines and valleys of the floral cotton sheet that surrounded her.

'You making sport,' I said. 'You know what you're doing? You're breaking up our family, that's what you're doing. We're a family!'

'We pretend to be a family (and you don't have to shout). We pretended for a long time. No, you go on to Savannah. Me and the girls staying right here.'

'I should've known,' I said, my voice low, bitter and cruel. 'That's what she called you 'bout today, right? Your mother never liked me.' My words slapped her, so she turned her back on them. 'She never did. And now she want to take you all from me. Damn!'

'My mother ain't got nothing to do with this,' she said, still turned away from me. 'This is my decision. *My* decision.'

When my weight settled on the bed, Simone spun fiercely around.

'Alphonso, what you doing?'

'I understand how you feel...'

'No, you don't. I don't think so.'

'Really, Simone,' I said inching toward her, 'I love...'

'Don't even try that,' she said, recoiling from my reach and turning her back again.

'OK, OK, OK,' I said. 'I see.' No sooner had my weight lifted from the bed than I plunged my hand under the sheet and under Simone's night gown. My full weight re-entered the bed, and I began kneading her buttocks.

'No!' she shouted, pushing me away. 'Don't touch me!' She was livid with rage and kept turned away from me. But when she didn't get up off the bed at once, I seized my chance and began slowly, gently, massaging her neck. Her response was slow but encouraging. I did this all the time and knew she liked it. I could feel the tension lessening in her neck, her shoulders. Her resistance was fading under my touch. Her guard toppled to the floor under my patient, trustworthy hands. These were the hands she had fallen in love with and had married. Before long, my hand had slid inside her black silk panties, and there was nothing anyone could do to stop it. Slowly I rolled over on top of her, my confident mouth seeking hers, finding it. She felt me, felt a rush of passion and lust and involuntarily drew me in.

I moved as if seeking a response I was being denied. But for all the whirling stars and volcanic rushes, I knew, with a conviction deeper than involuntary pleasure, that Simone had made up her mind. She would begin preparing Lucinda and Denise for the eventual separation. She would be honest with them, let them know that it wasn't their fault, that it was Daddy's decision to move to Savannah, that both Mommy and Daddy loved them dearly, and that her staying in Martinez was best for them. They would no longer have to be changing schools, no longer have to be constantly changing friends, and Mommy would be able to settle into her career and be happy. I couldn't blame her, and I wouldn't harbour any resentment. She'd do what I had driven her to do. She had no other choice but to leave me. But I couldn't bear the thought of losing my children. I didn't know if I could live with that. I remembered the words of an island poet, one of whose books we owned. The poet, with an acute sense of loss, had squatted outside a Finley Fish and Chips in London, dreaming of stability and of returning home, and thinking: *It was the only chance/ to rediscover my true root/ and branch and singing leaf.*

CHAPTER TWO

Yesterday I had pleaded yet again, 'Come with me, Simone, come with me.'

'It's too late, Alphonso,' she had replied. 'We ain't moving with you. Not this time. Not ever again.'

'But I need you,' I'd implored, looking up from a carton half-filled with books. 'I need my family.' I stood up and rested a hand on the bookcase. I felt as though I was choking from a fog that had been creeping into me over the past few months. Kindness had allowed her to help me with the packing, but the resolute look on her face told me her heart was sure.

'I just can't figure you out,' she had said. Slowly shaking her braided head from side to side, she'd removed the last painting from the wall of the upstairs office and started to wrap it. It was one of her acrylics (done when she was an undergraduate art minor) of five featureless women, whose gestures suggested conversation, sitting under a sprawling pecan tree. 'I figured when we moved to Florence, with the promotion and all, you'd settle down. I figured you'd say: "Well, look at that. I've been promoted. I'm living large now." But, no. You had to keep moving. It's over, Alphonso. It was over the day Lucinda's diarrhoea spells started. You can go wherever you want to. We're staying right here. I'll get a job. I'll raise my kids without you and your sorry rootlessness.'

She continued wrapping the painting as she spoke, not once looking at me. A sea of helplessness covered me. I squatted, wordless, and pushed the books in the carton in front of me firmly up against each other.

'I'm just as afraid of anarchy as you are, Simone,' I finally said. 'Trust me.'

'Are you kidding?' she said. An overweight silence elbowed its way between us and settled with a frown. She leaned the now wrapped painting against the wall and, moving slowly toward the staircase, she answered herself: 'Boy, are you kidding.' I snapped my guilt-ridden head away from her sarcasm and glanced through the window to see Lucinda and Denise dashing about the yard in a chasing game. The thought of losing them horrified me. Had Simone told them everything? It didn't look so. Either she had told them nothing or she had thoroughly prepared them for this day. I bit my lip, thinking of all the instability I had caused. I felt as if I deserved the guilt, the punishment of guilt, and, as I lowered my head, I willingly absorbed the bad feelings generated by Simone's caustic response. Yet, even up to yesterday, nothing, not even separation from my family, however horrific that thought had been, had begun to change my mind about moving, or to push me to break from the habits that had trapped me over the years.

My employers, Wesslar Aluminium, would normally have paid my moving expenses, including packing, but that was only if they had transferred me. The opportunity for transfers, every two or three years, was one of the attractions of my job as an engineer. But the last move in 1995 from Florence, South Carolina, to Martinez (our longest sojourn (almost a year and a half), and my impending one to Savannah had been requested by me and the moving expenses were therefore my own responsibility. Long before the last move I'd been more than aware of Simone's frustrations but felt powerless to do anything about them.

My own compulsions were, it seemed, far stronger. I understood their sources. Moving freed me from the pressure of buying a house in the U.S., gave me the excuse of being too busy to visit Barbados, despite Simone's constant urging. I wasn't ready either to fully commit to America or to confront my feelings towards my deceased parents and brother Elroy. Given all this, I lacked the will, the emotional energy to release those around me from the disorienting effects of my perennial relocations.

I'd lived in America for so many years and still Barbados squatted always on the crust of my consciousness. My dreams were peopled with the friends of my working-class youth, the slow-paced simple living, the games we played: road tennis, with a court drawn in the road with a chalky stone, plywood rackets, a ten-inch high piece of deal board across the court's centre for a net; bottle cricket, where we knelt instead of stood up to play, three soda drink bottles for stumps, a ball made from newspaper, wetted, rolled, and knitted with cord; road cricket, a vertical rectangular piece of wood, propped at the back with a thin piece of wood or a tree branch for stumps, and tennis balls for bowling; fowl cock: where we hooked the beaks of dried quarters of mahogany pods and tried to break our opponent's beak by the swiftness and force of our tugging.

My dreams rode on surf each night, through sparkling water where tails of sunlight wriggled over the sea-bed's white sand. My memory was lodged on that distant palm-ringed shore where casuarinas bent against the wind but never broke, where the sun cast its zinc glare equally on the sea's roof and the roofs of chattel houses. My dreams lurched with startled cries like a lay-floater who inadvertently drifts into a patch of anemones and feels himself being encircled by their restless hands pulling him under.

★   ★   ★

Now, as I watched Simone descend the staircase, I studied her profile as if seeing her for the first time: the size eight, five-foot nine figure, which made her two inches taller than me; the curves of that figure; the jet-black braided hair; the widow's peak; the chocolate-brown complexion compared to my light caramel; the slow uncoiling walk; the round buttocks that made men stare and sweat but which, today, seemed only to roll with unhappiness. In her *Reeboks*, stone-washed denims, and a pink T-shirt she intersected a path of ochre light that had cut through the sash window and knifed past her down the stairs. She held the rails as she descended, accompanied by the shadow of her girlish exuberance. For a long time now, she had stopped calling me 'Honey' or 'Sweetheart' or 'Darlin'. All those endearments had changed to 'Alphonso', a laboured, bladed 'Alphonso'.

This had been gradual at first but, somewhere around the move to Florence, the face of disillusionment had shown itself. She had good cause. My nomadic compulsions had undoubtedly blighted her career as a state social worker. Starting and stopping jobs so frequently did not endear her to her superiors. The manifestation of discontent came in the form of her plunge into the activities of the Baptist church which she attended each Sunday with the children. Her involvement included chairing the Fine Arts Committee and participating as a member of the Women's League and the Missionary Outreach and Home Help Committees. I, too, had a religious upbringing but, since my mid-teens, had never seriously followed any religion. I guess I was an agnostic. I would, however, accompany Simone and the girls to church at Easter, Christmas, and for the Mother's Day and Father's Day programs. I did this out of a sense of duty and would sit through the services, blank and neutral, sometimes thinking about work or even the pleasure I gained from polishing my car. For the most part, I reacted to Simone's spiritual excursions with something

18

like bemused contempt. I felt she was deliberately using these involvements as a weapon against me, as a means of avenging the frustrations of which she believed me to be the cause. And, even though I wouldn't admit to it, she was right. Each year of our marriage, the moving took place. It first triggered and then maintained our estrangement. Perhaps it was my pride or my ignorance, but I could not bring myself to admit to her I was to blame. I could not let her win.

'Anyone would think you're the preacher or the preacher's wife, the amount of time you spend out there,' I told her one Saturday last year. 'I don't trust any of those pastors. They're all the same: lecherous, materialistic....' I rubbed in my criticisms with mounting pleasure.

'Is your-anti-sermon over yet?' she said brusquely.

'Listen... you and your pastor ain' the only ones who can preach, you know.'

Simone tightened her face and said, 'Ever since you finished grad school, you've been on my case. I'm tired telling you that perhaps you should go home for a holiday. You ain't acting right. Every year, all the moving.' She said the word 'moving' as if it were another woman competing for my affections. 'Forcing us to move every year ain't normal, Alphonso. It ain't normal and it ain't right.'

'Listen, Simone,' I said. 'You're always trying to control me, aren't you? Telling me what I should and should not do. I...am...not...predictable...and...you...can't...control...me. So stop trying to label me, OK?'

'I'm not trying to label you, Alphonso. I actually love your sorry ass. I'm just trying to understand you. I thought I did when we got married.' She looked bewildered, the look of one hurt by the shock of such misunderstanding. Her judgment was in question. Her face filled with question marks and disbelief. I could see her anguish but made no effort to relieve it. If I had, I feared I would have invited scrutiny, and that I was resolutely on guard against. So I remained smug and stolid behind my mask of self control. Macho mask. Mask of pride. I felt safe. I felt protected.

'Why don't you take us all to Barbados for a holiday?' Simone was getting too close again. I braced for my well-rehearsed denial. In her eyes, a forest of sadness was growing. 'Perhaps seeing where you were born would help me understand you better.'

'No!' I shouted, warding off the encroaching ghosts. 'That's out of the question right now.' How often and in how many different situations had I erected the barrier of secrecy, hammering the nail heads firmly around my past?

'So, Alphonso,' she said with a look of helplessness and fatigue, 'what is it you want?'

'Nothing.'

'Nothing,' she repeated with a sigh. 'Look, I'm only trying to help. I'm not trying to dominate you. Just trying to help.' Her last words were spoken in all but a whisper, as a prayer or cry for help.

I said, 'I don't know, Simone. Perhaps this urge to move so often is hereditary. As I once told you, my dad was a driver most of his adult life. He went from one driving job to another. All his life. Perhaps I got to thinking this was the best way to be, to embrace the newness of varying locations. Isn't change enriching, Simone? Doesn't it keep one from getting complacent? Make life less dull?'

'Change can be good, Alphonso. But ours is way too frequent, disturbingly frequent…. Remember the saying about the rolling stone? You have a family now, Alphonso. Commitments…'

* * *

That particular conversation had come some weeks after my Aunt Lolita (who had emigrated to New York from Barbados) had pressed me to go home to see about my parent's house which she had been looking after. Simone, too, had seized the opportunity to press me. She told me again that not having gone back to Barbados to attend my parents' funeral must have been psychologically damaging and that I should go now.

'Better late than never,' she'd said. 'You'd feel better. Although you've stopped talking about it, I know you still feel guilty about their deaths. The more reason to go, Alphonso. Create a feeling of closure. You'll feel better.'

Their urgings were to no avail. I feigned a passionate disinterest in owning property as a way of not having to explain myself or, rather, as a perfect explanation for not wanting to go to Barbados and for not owning my own property in America.

My feelings about my parents' deaths (and my brother Elroy's) and my reluctance to deal with them were like writhing sea anemones that had long stirred in me. Simone's decision not to move with me to Savannah, coupled with the imminent threat of losing my two daughters, had widened the crack in the lid of my past. For the past few weeks the pent-up spirits had danced in circles around me, challenging me to rise as a hero and put them to rest. Still I couldn't do it. If I'd been able to act, I'd have purchased a house years ago. I loved investments and felt property to be the best kind. But I was no hero. I felt as if the spirits were taunting me, laughing at me. And I was afraid of them. Moving had allowed me temporary respite from them, but they'd catch up with me again. Were they spirits of the damned or the blessed? I needed some sign. I didn't have the strength or courage to face them.

★   ★   ★

How I created diversions from such moments, when Simone got too close, was both inexcusable and shameful.

'Who left this magazine on the table?' I'd demand, or 'Yesterday, there were at least two books put in backwards in the bookcase. What's going on, man? What's going on?'

The force of my voice hammered the house, and the children cowered. I knew what these performances were about but felt powerless to prevent them.

'Was it you, Lucinda?'

Lucinda frowned miserably and said, 'I was looking at the pictures. I was just looking at the pictures.' She stood there with her hair bunched in two at the sides and curled in a muff at the front, ready to cry. Near the staircase, Denise adjusted the dress on one of her dolls. A lancing guilt tried to penetrate my anger.

'I was reading the magazine,' Simone said, rescuing Lucinda. She briskly ushered the girls up the stairs.

'And you ups and just left it there? Damn!'

I stomped out of the house, slamming the door behind me as I entered the garage. The November rain had taken a two-day break, and I had decided to take advantage of the sky's clarity. I took the red Nissan onto the driveway, got out and placed an empty plastic bucket on the ground under the engine.

I jacked up the car, slid under it, and disengaged the oil drainage plug. Some of the oozing black fluid spilled over my hand before I could remove it. While trying to get the hand out of the way, the plug escaped my grasp and sank into the oily depths. The car had not been driven all morning, so the oil was cool. I probed the sludge and retrieved the plug. Then I buried my hand in the towel next to me and slid out from under the car. Wiping my hands clean, I looked up into the limpid blue sky. I began to feel better, though when a cardinal, in raging red, dipped low over the yard speaking a harsh language, it sounded not dissimilar to my wife when we fell into the mire of misunderstanding. When the bucket was full, I removed it from under the car and took it into the garage where I emptied its contents into a three-foot high plastic container kept there for that purpose. Simone opened the side door which led to the garage just as I was doing this.

'Alphonso, I told you not to raise your fucking voice at my children,' she hissed with uncharacteristic profanity. 'You know how it affects them, especially Lucinda. She's having diarrhoea again and her school work hasn't been improving.'

'I'm sorry,' I said. Her words cut through me and turned in my bowels. Guilt billowed inside me. But as I emptied the oil, I maintained a calm and composed expression. I couldn't let her see where my weakness lay or the bit of oil that had spilled on to the garage floor when her mouth had sliced me in half, and over which I now calmly placed my right foot. By now, a large lump had gathered in my throat. Lucinda was our first child. Daddy's girl. I knew she was having great difficulty in adjusting to the migrancy which had become our lifestyle. Particularly over the last two years, her school grades had been declining, and her frowning discontent had started to rub off on the younger Denise. I knew I was hurting my family but felt powerless to change. So I willed myself to swallow the difficult lump.

'I'll talk with her,' I said.

'You need to do more than that, damn you. I'm going to leave you, Alphonso. I swear to God I'm going to leave.'

'Tell her I'm coming in soon.' The pitch of my voice had dropped considerably. The guilt lump, while not digested, had been swallowed. This allowed a wind of seduction to gush up through my wind pipe, and I felt an old confidence blowing in me. How long this would last, I couldn't tell. I would win her back. I would win my wife back. The inner wind prodded me forward, but, as I approached Simone, she flailed both arms in the air to ward me off.

'Don't touch me,' she hissed. 'Don't you touch me.'

'I'm sorry, Baby. I'm sorry,' I said, grabbing her wrists. She fought to break my grip.

'Alphonso, you're hurting me.'

I immediately released her. I passed my right hand over my head, shook my head, sighed heavily. Simone was shuddering and tearful.

'What's happened to us?' she asked. 'When was the last time we laughed?'

'I don't know,' I said. 'All I know is that I love you. I love and need my family.'

Simone sucked in her top lip, no doubt conveying her feelings about the regularity with which this scene was played.

'Tell Lucinda I'll be in soon.'

'OK.' The hiss was out of her voice. Her softened face indicated some relief. This became clearer when she broached a new subject. 'What you plan to do with all that old oil?'

I replied that, as yet, I was still inquiring as to what agency would be able to collect the three-foot high container.

'It wouldn't be environmentally conscious to put it in the trash or pour it in the ground somewhere,' I said, walking slowly back to my car. Then I heard the side door close. The careful click of the lock indicated a truce. A temporary but welcome truce.

When I had taken off the old oil filter and attached a new one, I lowered the car and packed away the tools. Then I poured four quarts of new oil into the engine. I took the empty bottles behind the house where I carefully placed each one in the recycling container. As I returned to the car, a piece of the foil covering from one of the oil bottles glinted at me. How could I have missed this? I seized this little emblem of disorder and imprecision, and placed it with the rest of the oil bottles in the container behind the house.

Later that evening I took the girls to Macs. My darlings. I took them outside to the play park and watched them jump up and down in the ball pen, watched as they screamed down the slides and bucked the stationary horses. Inside, they laughed and giggled with hands fastened to hamburgers and cokes. I laughed with them. I bit their hamburgers and made faces. When we got home, I made sure they flossed and, after a brief conversation with their mother, I tucked them into bed. I stood by the doorway for, it seemed, a very long time, watching them, contented now, snuggled under the sheets with their teddy bears.

I knew all along that Simone's efforts to figure me out were motivated by love, but I still couldn't bring myself to let her in to my island past. My feelings, particularly about Elroy, I was not ready to share. So I had to wear whatever mask was necessary in order to prevent the possibility of revelation. Mask of anger. Mask of accusation. Macho mask. I desperately wanted to return to Barbados for a visit, to put flesh on my dreams of surf. Yet I kept putting it off. In the end, I would decide not to go. These juxtaposing desires followed me everywhere, and it seemed impossible to be rid of them.

Before marriage, life seemed so much simpler, and I was happy. I studied, socialized with Simone, got good grades. I realized later that all these activities had merely been temporary lids to cap the stirrings deep inside me, stirrings that I knew intimately but found impossible to publicly name. It was the unabated guilt over not attending my parents' funeral in 1984, and the haunting of my mysterious elder brother, Elroy, that still swirled those restless anemones. Simone knew something of my guilt over not attending the funeral, and she knew of my parents' house which Aunt Lolita was managing. After I'd told her how badly I felt about having been away when my parents died, I began to feel like a whiner. Simone consoled me as best as she could, but still the feelings remained. Perhaps I should have sought some professional help. Perhaps I hadn't been fully honest with myself about my feelings towards my parents. But my deepest fear was telling her about Elroy. I didn't know all the facts surrounding Elroy's illness. All I knew was that he had been paralysed from birth and had been institutionalized all his life in a home for the mentally and physically handicapped called Gracewood. Would Simone understand? Would she conclude that there was some hereditary bad blood in my line that could suddenly one day alter one of the girls or a child of the future? I was not going to let Simone know about Elroy, and the burden of this secrecy came between us. I was now one step back from her, making room for Elroy's ghost.

'Are you seeing someone, Alphonso?' Simone would ask. But when I told her I wasn't, she would say to an invisible auditor in the room, 'I want my husband back. Whoever or whatever you are, I want my husband back.'

CHAPTER THREE

One of the first things I'd packed when I'd started a couple of days ago was my Gibson acoustic guitar. It lay in a coffin-like case whose lid was lined in yellow velvet. I'd once had aspirations to being a West Indian pop star. During high school, I saved all the extra change from my allowances to purchase my first guitar, an Edmond. I even did a number of gigs: hotels, house parties, a few at Alexandra's, a prestigious Swedish-owned club, a few at the Tamarind Cove Hotel. I remembered my first performance at Tamarind Cove and the audience's lukewarm response. After the performance, the British owner, a short plump and ruddy man in his forties who always wore suspenders, insisted that the tourists wanted to hear West Indian standards and not the original music I was giving them. They wanted to hear traditional folk songs like the ones heard in the tourist promotional videos such as 'Yellow Bird', 'Jamaica Farewell', 'Beautiful Barbados', and 'Island in the Sun'. I told him I was a serious artist and wanted to give visitors a fresh view of the island. He looked at me as if I were mad, his cheeks flushed over, his congeniality vanished. I was to give him what he wanted. I was working for him. I said nothing and wasn't surprised when the next week and all other weeks afterwards, he didn't call for my services. It was then I finally accepted what my friend Clarence Browne had been telling me all along. *If you doan sing 'Yellow Bird' for them, they goin' make your arse shite.*

All over the island, there seemed to be this hostility toward originality. And not just from tourists but from Barbadians as well. I recalled the fate of the singing duo, The Draytons Two. They had created rhythms uniquely their own, spouge (a fusion of Barbadian folk, reggae, and rhythm and blues) and, later they had built on tuk with its fusions of English marching band and African drum rhythms. But the locals did not buy enough Draytons Two records to make production viable for the recording company and eventually, and perhaps inevitably, like Jackie Opel before them, they faded into obscurity. I concluded that it was impossible to pursue art seriously on the island and opted for an engineering career instead. I did continue to play my guitar for relaxation and recreation and, every now and again, I'd purchase a new one. The current Gibson Epiphone was three years old.

I had not made fast progress with the packing. My attention frequently drifted, to the past, to the view out of the window, to the line of dogwood trees that marshal the back yard, leaves turning ochre, and behind them the taller trees – pecan, ash, pine – that punctuate the lot. I'd look for Lucinda and Denise playing in the garden, catch sight of an occasional squirrel, quick as a shadow, scurrying along the moss-carpeted branches. I felt utterly lost and alone.

It was when I'd finally got my attention back to the packing that I'd rediscovered *The Volcanoes of Sao Paulo* (by someone called Jeremy Bishop). As I pulled out the book from its case, a small brown flake fell to the floor, and I grimaced at the sight of the severed leg or partial wing of a long-dead cockroach. I reached over to the oak desk and withdrew two napkins from their floral box. With the napkins as gloves, I picked up the disgusting crust and with a single toss, threw it and the tissues into the blue plastic trash can in the corner. I returned to the book and smiled to myself at the colourful painting on the front cover. In the left foreground, a bronzed Spanish-looking man with loosened tie, gripped his left elbow with his right hand. His white shirt was torn across the left shoulder revealing a nasty gash from which blood spilled all over the shirt and down to the hurricane-gray slacks. In the right foreground, a deep-sea fisherman was hauling in a shark. Had the dark-tanned man been thrown overboard from some vessel and been bitten by a shark? Had he accidentally fallen overboard? Was he a friend of the fisherman? Or was he enemy? What was the relationship between the two scenes? I began reading Chapter One:

> THE BOEING 747 bored like a lonely silver fish through the cloudless afternoon sky. The sea's horizon and the sky had fused together making it impossible to tell one from the next. All the visible world had become a single colour: blue.

I continued skimming, trying to recall the story. It appeared that the plane was on a mission to Sao Paulo to investigate the circumstances of a missing aircraft whose British crew and passengers were presumed dead. This was the second crash in one and a half years and the airline had lost a lot of its reputation as a result of the bad publicity. Its officials desperately wanted to restore its good name. It was Quinn (presumably the handsome, wounded cover hero) whose job it was to solve the puzzle of the missing plane.

My attention drifted. I had not kept the book for its story. I thought again of Simone's puzzlement each time I announced my decision to move, and of my own bewilderment. Bewilderment because, although I could explain my compulsion, I felt crippled to stop it. I knew our frequent moves had a negative impact on my family. I knew that people in the army moved around a lot, but (as Simone frequently pointed out) everyone involved expected that.

Whilst my job involved transfers, I had pushed this moving beyond normalcy. Lucinda had to change schools and, where commuting was impossible, Simone had to look for new jobs. As a state social worker, transfers were not the norm for her. How would any prospective employer view such apparent instability?

★ ★ ★

'The way we move is a big joke at the office,' Simone said during the last of our eight moves. 'And wait till I tell my mama. Mama's really gonna pitch a fit this time.'

That move had been eight hundred miles away to another state. Lucinda was five years old then; Denise, just three. Mrs. Williams' darlings. With the many moves within Louisiana (North Baton Rouge to Shreveport, New Orleans, South Baton Rouge, LaFayette, Lake Charles, South-West Baton Rouge), Mrs. Williams could still see her darlings, if only at weekends in some cases. She and Mr. Williams, a retired clerk in an engineering firm and a local district politician, would arrive in Mr. Williams's large brown Lincoln town car to see their darlings. For Mrs. Williams, this included her youngest daughter as well.

'Let her,' I said. I could feel my tongue burning with mischief. 'That's the trouble with you Americans. You try to run other people's lives. You guys have become the watchdogs of the world.'

'Watch your tongue, Mister,' Simone said, falling into my web. 'Don't you be calling my mother no dog.'

'It's just a figure of speech, Da'ling,' I said. My silent inner laughter now gushed up and leapt loudly out of my mouth. I had successfully gotten under her skin. 'Don't be so highty-tighty. Come. Gi' de man a hug, nuh.' My words bubbled in the air, but Simone didn't share my levity.

'I'm tired,' she said, slowly and irritably removing my hand from around her waist. 'All this moving has me tired.'

30

'Well, it won't be for long, Sugar. This is the big one. It's promotion time, *yes*.' I placed a strong relishing stress on the word 'yes.' After eight years in the engineering business, I'd finally made senior supervisor.

'Perhaps now we won't have to move so often, huh?' Simone said. 'You know how unsettling it is for the kids.'

'Definitely,' I said.

Six months had passed in Florence and Simone still hadn't gotten a job. That was when she decided to resurrect her artistic interests, having been an Art minor in college. She had painted off and on since then, but nothing as serious as this. Just as she had done with the church activities, she again plunged into a world that excluded me, a world which seemed to bring her some joy. I ought to have felt better to see her like this, for I was painfully aware that she acquired no joy through me, but that was not how I responded.

– We can't afford not to have two incomes.

– It's better than nothing. I have to do something with myself.

– Do something with yourself?

– I can't keep a job with us moving as we do. I'm plain tired having to hunt for a job every time we move.

– You gave up too soon.

– What?

– You gave up too soon. This is too much on me.

– My work's been selling. I contribute to the expenses.

– Yes, but we don't have any extras like we used to.

– And whose fault is that? You destroyed that, Alphonso. The moving destroyed all that. You've destroyed your family, and you don't even realize it.

– Don't say that, baby. Please don't say that.

– I'm saying it 'cause it's true. Until you deal with whatever keeps you on the run, things'll only get worse. Why you so afraid to visit your homeland? Doing that may be what you need.

– Don't tell me what I do and do not need.

– I didn't mean it like that, Alphonso. Have you any idea how unstable you are and how unstable this family has become? I said no more, because I knew she was right. I felt what seemed like thousands of sea anemones stirring in me.

* * *

I was still holding the book. I couldn't remember what happened to the missing crew and passengers or whether Quinn solved the mystery, and now I would never know. Three pages into Chapter Two, and the book took on the coffin-like aspect of the guitar case. The front cover and the first nineteen pages were a lid on the rectangular cutout that went deep into the next two hundred and forty pages. The borders of these pages were stuck together with glue, leaving only a few loose pages at the back of the book. With the book closed, it was impossible to detect the cut out pages. The space contained three air-letter forms, two from my Aunt Lolita and one from my deceased father, Fitzgerald. My father's was postmarked, Maryland, U.S.A., dated 1977 and addressed to me at 50 Liverpool Road, Redman's Land, St. Michael, Barbados. Aunt Lolita's were postmarked Bridgetown, Barbados, 1984 and 1985 respectively and addressed to me at P.O. Box 14365, Louisiana State University, Baton Rouge, LA 70803.

Underneath the letters was a pay slip dated the 26th of July, 1980. It had my name on it under the employee section. Employer, the Barbados Library Service. Job status, clerical officer. Thoughts were racing before me now like sea swifts or gusts of wind made visible on the surface of the water. This pay slip had been issued on my first full-time job during the year between high school and my departure for the United States. This was the same year that I had pursued my pop star fantasy by performing in several hotels and clubs on the island.

It was in the Library Service that I first met Clarence Browne, the only person in Barbados with whom I was still in touch, albeit sporadically. When I first left the island, I had done most of the corresponding. I hadn't taken Clarence's lack of response personally, for it was generally accepted that West Indians at home were very undependable letter writers. After a while, I got tired of the one-sidedness of the communication with the inevitable result that Clarence and I hardly wrote to each other any more. Once or twice a year, we'd telephone each other. These were relatively brief calls.

We had hit it off really well at the start. Clarence was a struggling novelist and I a struggling musician. Our clerical posts took care of our basic needs, but as avid and eclectic readers we were both aware of a larger world outside the island, a consciousness that produced in us a sense of simultaneous hope and despair.

'Twenty focking years in de Civil Service and nothing to show for it,' Clarence said, biting into a fried chicken leg at our favourite corner table at the Pink Pelican. We were on our lunch break. His upper body came forward like a rushing sigh and his right foot leapt out involuntarily as if a doctor had tapped his knee. His foot capsized the chair next to him, which clattered as it fell across the cement floor. Clarence sucked his teeth and scooped the chair back into a standing position with his foot. Then he bit into the chicken again. 'Listen to me, Alphonso,' he said between chewing and swallowing. 'I'm at least twenty years older than you. Get to fock outta dis island, you hear what I tell you? Forget Barbados.'

'You don't think things'll change?' I knew when Clarence's temper simmered like this to avoid making any statements. My role was to feed him questions in reply to which he could eventually exorcize his rage.

'Shite, man. When I think of Cuba with its Casa de Las

33

Americas and the publishing outlets further afield (New York, London) dis place does make my arse hurt. I sorry as shite I didn't get out when I was younger, man. You can try with your music, man, but if you ain' prepared to sing *Yellow Bird*, your arse goin' see stars.'

'You might be right,' I said, still surprised by his intensity. 'But I can still give it a shot – at least for a few years.'

'How old you are now?' Clarence asked, his forehead etched with wavelike furrows.

'Eighteen.'

'You got youth on your side, Brother-man. And maybe things'll work out for you.' I knew he was hurting. I knew the rage masked his pain, and I had to encourage him.

'So how's the novel coming along?'

'All right. I just need to get an agent...'

'Sounds like a really good story, man. George Washington sowing his wild oats in Barbados when he came down here wid he sick brother. How long you said he was down here?'

'A year or so. Was de only time he ever travel outta de States.'

'And how old you say he did?'

'Around your age so.'

'If that novel gets published, man, the government goin' declare you *persona non grata*. It'll ruin the tourist trade, man.'

'Ruin the tourist trade? Don't mek sport. On the contrary...' Clarence's eyes were twinkling. His dark mood had changed. '... it may very well *increase* the trade. Heh, heh, heh. Some Americans may want to get some of what Georgie-Porgie got.'

'And what's that?' I asked, reeling in his light-heartedness.

'What's that? You mean you don't know?' Clarence sucked his teeth, delaying his punch line for dramatic effect. 'Man, Georgie-Porgie got de clap, man. He got de frigging clap.'

The two of us fell into loud uninhibited laughter. I kept slapping the table top and holding onto it as if to prevent myself from collapsing. Clarence sat back, his legs wide open and a satisfied grin on his face. His cheeks twitched and his well-oiled Adam's apple rose and fell. Some of the Pink Pelican patrons stared at us, while others looked on with curiosity. A few people, infected by our merriment, joined in the laughter. The chubby, head-tied owner of the restaurant waddled over to our table.

'You boys real happy today.'

'Nothing else to be,' Clarence replied.

'You want anything else?'

'Nah,' I said. I believed the crafty proprietor was really checking us out to ensure nothing illegal was going on at the boisterous table, like the use of drugs, which were easily acquired on Baxters Road where the restaurant was situated.

I looked at the pay slip again. My monthly salary then was seven hundred and fifty Barbados dollars or approximately three hundred and seventy-five U.S. dollars. I was now earning four thousand U.S. dollars gross pay. The thought of this financial success made a smile stretch across my face. If only my mum and dad had been alive to see me now. They would have been proud. They had taught me more than they knew, and I regretted not telling them how much I appreciated them while they were alive. My grief and guilt rose in the knowledge that nothing could be changed. I couldn't believe in any grand encounter in an afterlife where loved ones recognized each other and reminisced and righted all wrongs. So I was left in my sea of regret. At the time of their deaths, Simone had comforted me as best she could by saying my parents wouldn't want me to spend the rest of my life in guilt over them, that they'd want only for me to be happy. Her words brought some encouragement, some relief, but my old feelings would invariably rise again and break the surface of my peace. Underneath the pay slip were two four-by-two-inch brown envelopes. These once contained half-ounces of marijuana. Little flecks of the weed still clung to the sticky flaps of the envelopes. Two packets of Rizla Red lay next to the envelopes. One packet was part used; the other unused. I remembered rolling the joints in these. I no longer smoked marijuana, but I'd briefly experimented during my fifteenth year. I fingered the contents of the paper tomb again: the letters, pay slip, envelopes, cigarette paper. They felt like pieces of myself buried (alive or dead) like the crew and passengers of the missing craft.

Were the enclosed fragments the voices from my past calling me to confront the instability that was ravaging my life? Were they fragments or bones through which, if I could muster the will, my life could be reassembled and revised? Could they still the anemones inside me, bring me rest from my constant movement?

It wasn't that I didn't have rational reasons for not buying a house here. It felt too much like an admission of total acceptance of America and a simultaneous severing of all ties with Barbados. I couldn't have that. I had already gone far enough by becoming a U.S. citizen in 1992. I hadn't wanted to do this, but had felt forced into it after George Bush's government tightened the 1990 immigration laws. No longer would permanent residency status be permanent. Now, after every ten years, one had to reapply for another ten-year extension. This was too much of an inconvenience, so I went ahead and applied for citizenship and was sworn in, December 12, 1992. And this new U.S. status, which let me keep my Barbados passport active, was as far as I would go. To seal this commitment to America by purchasing a home here felt like irrevocably choosing adoption over nativity. As I continued looking at the fragments, I'd grown progressively disoriented and excited by the prospect of conquering my past. I'd felt simultaneously pulled towards the harbour of my birth, towards the Barbadian family I had lost, and towards the American family I was about to lose; and guilt-ridden over both. I stared, as a man in limbo, into the paper tomb, into the fragments, for clues.

CHAPTER FOUR

I took out my father's letter from the hollowed-out novel and started to read:

Dear Alphonso:

I coming back home in another few weeks.

The six months in Maryland with the Farm Labor Program didn't too bad. Hard work but the money will come in handy for your school books and things and also to repair the house. Those godforsaken termites will eat a man out of house and home. Don't forget to spray the Chlordane round the house once a month, hear?

You keep asking 'bout Elroy. Don't let that keep worrying you, son. As you know and as me and your mother always told you, your brother had something wrong wid him from the time he did born, a brain defect which caused de paralysis. We glad you never have to see him. We want to protect you from that, son. You wouldn't want to see him like that. I hope you well, in the name of the Lord, and that you studying you school work good. You know, if I had de opportunities like you, I woulda been a doctor or lawyer or somebody big today. So you keep working hard and don't forget to pray and read your Bible. God bless you, son.

Your nice dad.

See Elroy like what? It was the question that had haunted me for the five years before receiving this letter, since the time, when I was ten, I had first learnt of his existence. Elroy must have been nearly twenty-one at the time. I picture myself lying on the green and beige living room sofa, hands clasped behind my head, staring into the asbestos ceiling.

My eyes land on a hole, about the size of a stove knob, which had been chiselled by rats. I imagine Elroy's body collapsed like a flag. The face I put on it was from a photograph of Elroy as a baby. The photo didn't hang on a wall, nor was it standing in a frame on top the Zenith black and white television set or on the mahogany chest of drawers. I had inadvertently come upon it while fingering through Tennyson's *In Memoriam* and had inquired about the smiling child. He had my light caramel complexion, but his cheeks were larger than mine, his hair more matted. Was it a relative? A cousin perhaps? I asked my parents one day during dinner. I remember the long silence, the looks that asked which-one-of-us-will-speak-first? I was ten years old and guessed that my parents couldn't risk lying to me at that age.

''Tis your elder brother, son,' my father finally said.

'My brother? How come nobody told me I had a brother?'

'Your brother has been hospitalized since he did born. So he don't stay with us. We can't look after him.'

'Can I see him?'

'No,' my parents collectively said.

''Tis better if you don't see he the way he is. I don't want you worrying.'

'We want you to concentrate on you schoolwork and mek a good life for youself,' my mother said, eyes welling with tears. 'Elroy in God's hands.'

That smiling chubby-faced child stayed with me all through the years. It was as though time had frozen Elroy's face, but his body was deflated, shrivelled. Chubby chinless

39

face on an emaciated body. An old man. A child. A playmate for me in the absence of a real one. I had to make it real. I had a brother whom I had never actually seen and whom I was not allowed to see. When I was told of his existence, I married a baby face to twenty-one-year old body ravaged by paralysis. As grotesque as it seemed, this image was all I had of my brother. At least I had something.

I picture myself when I first received my father's letter, pressing it to my chest with a slightly trembling hand, the vast quietness of the house engulfing me. The battery-operated wall clock says five fifteen. In an hour or so, my mother is due home from the Simpsons, for whom she works as a maid. I get off the bed and go through the dining area where I accidentally strike my left thigh against the edge of the wrought-iron dining table. A sharp pain arches through my thigh, and followed by a duller, deeper pain and a numbness. I limp back into my room, rubbing my thigh as I go. Then I place the letter on the mahogany chest of drawers and turn to look out through the half-open window. The glazed leaves of the soursop tree are shaking reluctantly in the breeze and two small crows are arguing in the tree's balcony, squawking until they grow hoarse. Behind the tree, and facing eastward, are a row of houses from whose direction comes the muted sounds of car exhausts. Our house sits at the end of Liverpool Road, by the cul-de-sac, so it is relatively quiet. It only grows noisy during the night when stray dogs rule.

Lying on the bed, my eye would be drawn to a colored picture of a woman modelling underwear. I had cut out the picture from a magazine which I had borrowed from one of my friends. Mike, I think. I closely observe the outer fringes of the woman's breasts, which is all that can be seen, since her spread-out hands are pressed over them. My eyes slowly wander south to the white panty, trimmed at the waistline with lace that covered her navel. I wonder what the navel was like. Lowering my gaze still further, I observe the puffed-out pubic area and the wisp of black pubic hair protruding around the bottom line of the panties. No doubt, I would have felt a sudden pressure inside my pants.

Life-sized posters of Bob Marley clutching his guitar, loom from the room's two longer sides. I get up and put one of my Marley albums on the turntable of the red portable Sony combination player which my father had given me for my last birthday. I hoist the record arm to the track, 'No Woman No Cry'. The closing guitar solo cries with a longing so deep that it makes me want to walk through clouds, makes me want to run wild. I lie on the bed and stare at the ceiling.

The album ends, and I slide off the bed and go over to the deal-board bookcase which I had made at the age of twelve or thirteen. Used classical texts and popular novels which my mother had gotten from the Simpsons fill the shelves. The bookcase had been my first woodworking project after my father taught me how to saw wood. I remember him showing me how to grip the saw, keeping the forefinger pointing straight forward along the top side of the blade. The bookcase has four shelves and is thickly coated with black oil paint. I remove *The Volcanoes of Sao Paulo* from the shelf, open it, and place the letter in the secret compartment inside. I take out a small brown envelope and a packet of *Rizla-Reds*, and roll myself a joint. After fishing out a box of matches from the vanity drawer and lighting the spliff, I roll back onto the bed in a cloud of smoke, thinking of butter-flies and zebras and moonbeams and fairy tales.

I turn the player's selection switch to radio and listen to some rhythm and blues and calypso for about an hour or so. Then my stomach starts to make noises, and it suddenly occurs to me that I haven't eaten anything since coming home from school. My mother had cooked for me that morning and left the food in the refrigerator. When I got home I'd been so excited at receiving my father's letter, I hadn't, until now, thought about eating. No doubt, the ganja had also increased my appetite. So I fetch the dinner, heat it on the gas stove, and return to my room with it.

In another year, I would have to take the Ordinary Level Cambridge examinations, but my grades, I knew, were steadily dropping and I felt there was nothing I could do to stop the decline. Even in subjects such as Math, Physics, and Chemistry, to which I was naturally inclined, my test scores had become increasingly disappointing. Naturally, my parents were concerned over my last school report which showed me thirtieth out of a class of forty-five. This was a serious fall from grace, for I had never been placed lower than fourth before. I lacked motivation for school work, but there was no lack of interest for my music. My parents tried to encourage me, saying not to mind and that I would catch up. Somehow, their exhortations hadn't been enough to lift me. When, a few weeks later, the headmaster contacted my mother and informed her of my detentions for bad behaviour (the most serious instance being the verbal abuse of the Spanish teacher, Mr. Phillips), my mother had obviously informed my father. *I hope you well, in the name of the Lord, and that you studying you school work good...*

Along with Elroy's spectre, I think too that my family's incessant moving had made me pull into myself . (A sad irony, I now see. Do we ever learn from experience?) Before Redman's Land, we'd lived in Grazettes. Before that, Whitehall and Cave Hill and Jackson and Lodge Hill and Spooner's Hill. These moves had all taken place over a seven-year period, from my sixth to thirteenth year. Once a year during that period, I'd hear my father say to my mother, 'E? We need to get some more breathing space.' This was the reason my father always gave for the moving. It was true that the places where we'd lived were, invariably, neighbourhoods choked with chattel houses squatting just

42

a few feet apart. It was not uncommon to find one yard serving three households. Even when attempts were made to erect enclosures made of five-foot or six-foot high galvanized sheeting, these palings, as they were called, would gradually be flattened by the hands of mischievous children wanting freedom or breathing space. But the communities had been closely knit. Everybody knew everybody; doors and windows could be left wide open any time, day or night. With each move, I left friends I never found again. By the fifth departure, I had come to regard the moving as normal. Even though we'd been living at Redman's Land for two years now, I had become acutely aware of the pockets of emptiness which my father's nomadic tendencies appeared to have created in me. I lived with the constant anticipation of having to move again. And with each move, it seemed, my father took a new job as if in an effort to erase some part of his past and start a new life. And now he had gone to Maryland's corn and tobacco fields. *I hope you well in the name of the Lord and that you studying you schoolwork good... and don't forget to pray...*

Prayer seemed to be my parents' solution to everything. Sometimes, at night after they had retired and left me watching television, I could hear my father's gravel voice easing through the hardboard partition. He would be praying aloud. His tone was always very intimate and, initially, I would be startled to discover that it was the Unseen Guest (and not my mother) who was being addressed. Always, I would hear my name called, and Elroy's.

The praying made me very uneasy. Part of the reason for this was the guilt I felt for having stopped going to Sunday School under the excuse of having excessive homework. My parents were extremely disappointed with my decision, but they didn't force me to continue. I knew they were having difficulty knowing exactly how to deal with me. Of course, this wasn't their fault, although it would take me years to perceive this. They were both trying the best they knew how. Their lives, like their parents' (especially my mother's, I never knew my father's parents), were straightforward: serve God, raise a family, work and, in your spare time, raise a few chickens, a few sheep, cultivate a small kitchen garden, attend church socials, visit with family. I was dissatisfied with such simplicities. I was torn between a vision of myself as educated upper middle-class and the reality of my humble existence in a middle lower-class to lower-class neighbourhood. I wanted to be like the heroes in all those British and American novels I read in school or else be a rich and famous pop star like Bob Marley and have any girl I wanted.

School didn't make it any easier on me. I had what people called looks and this meant soft, curly hair and light-brown skin. I was also intellectually bright. This combination of looks and brightness endeared me to those students from the middle and upper classes whose parents were professional people: doctors, lawyers, nurses, teachers, government administrators, and such like. They all clamoured around me and, during school hours, I was something of a hero, excelling at everything I did. I was an athletic star, setting records in the hundred metres and the high jump, and equalling those in the two hundred metres and the long jump. It was said that I was a fearsome right-winger in the Under Sixteen soccer team. I became the Literary and Debating Society's most formidable debater and one of the top actors in the Drama Club.

My closest school friend, Christopher Riley, was the son of an officer at the Meteorological Institute. I would get a ride home on evenings with Mr. Riley, in his white Peugeot, when he came to collect Christopher. The Rileys lived somewhere in Christ Church, on the plush south coast, and had to pass near my neighbourhood on the way home. All this was pointed out by Mr. Riley when I tried to escape the offer with a stuttering, 'It's all right, Mr. Riley. I don't want to put you all out.' It was settled. For them. Not for me. Christopher, like all the other well-to-do students, felt that I was one of them. I had to find a way to prevent him from knowing that I lived in a small wooden house on a street where several of the neighbouring houses leaned embarrassingly or were half-devoured by termites. By the time we reached Redman's Land, I had found a solution. I told Mr. Riley that I lived just inside Liverpool Road, and so it was unnecessary for him to go to all the trouble of turning into the road. He could merely drop me off at the corner. This obviously sounded plausible to Mr. Riley and so, every evening, he would deliver me there at the corner, and I would walk the full length of Liverpool Road to my small wooden house by the cul-de-sac.

I lived in these two worlds, perpetually alert in my determination to keep my poverty a secret. I was angry with my parents for not having the means to make me middle-class. I back-chatted, went out without letting them know of my whereabouts, and was generally uncommunicative. Why couldn't my father have his own car instead of driving people all the time? I would sometimes find myself mentally shutting my parents out as if I could somehow will away my reality. At other times I grew confused, not knowing with whom I was really angry. I felt I couldn't talk to my parents about my feelings, because they wouldn't understand. They were both uneducated, in a conventional sense, and I was too immature to understand their simple and profound wisdom.

My father's mother died when he was three, and he was raised by aunts and uncles. His father, Archibald, an incurable womanizer, never married my father's mother and never looked out for his son. At thirteen, my father left school and learned tailoring, an apparently inherited skill. His mother was said to have been an excellent seamstress

45

and one of the prettiest women in her neighbourhood. But so dedicated was she to her work that she sat too long at the machine, which, over a period of time, caused her to develop stomach cramps and ulcers. These ailments led to chronic gastritis which claimed her life at the age of twenty-two. Her death was always with my father, journeying in his eyes like a cloud, mostly dark. He tailored for five years but when one of his uncles taught him how to drive, he decided that this was what he really wanted as his life's occupation. Perhaps motion and open spaces helped disperse the clouds of alienation which he felt. At eighteen, he began driving light goods vehicles for a number of city firms. Later, he drove molasses trucks for the Barbados Sugar Producers Corporation and soda drink trucks for a bottling company. When I was eight or nine, my father worked for the Transport Board as a driver of passenger buses.

I remembered that period with some fondness. We were living on Kings Road in Grazettes some twenty kilometres west of Redman's Land. It was the only time in my early youth I regarded my father with some pride. During the school holidays, my mother would fix his home-cooked lunch in a three-tiered enamel bowl, wrap it carefully in brown paper, put it in a leatherette bag, and give it to me to take to him. He worked the Whitehall bus route which ran just over the hill from Grazettes. I walked along Kings Road that ran like a grey ribbon in front of our house, and past Miss Browne's shop squatting on the corner where Kings intersected with Rockhampton. A street light at the intersection came on at exactly six o'clock each evening. Under the light, men and boys gathered for laughs, dominoes, and draughts.

Under this lamp post, a village character called 'Billy Graham' preached at any hour of the day or night. I remember once seeing him from a distance, his seven-foot praying mantis frame pacing in arcs under the street light. Waving his black Bible as if it were some kind of weapon, he strode, then halted abruptly, strode in another direction, then abruptly halted, like a horse trapped inside a corral. God's horse. Billy Graham preached on anything from the rascally behaviour of the neighbourhood's boys to the workings of island politics. He was never coherent, impossible to follow for any length of time. It was said that he was once a very educated man, a teacher, and that too much studying had addled his brain. He had several daughters and a son, all of whom did very well in school. One by one, after they had completed high school, the children emigrated to England, Canada and the U.S. to escape the embarrassment of their father, leaving the mother, a silent, private, fair-skinned woman, to bear the burden alone. But Billy Graham had become so much a part of the neighbourhood that no one ever actually felt threatened by him. He was part of the personality of the community. At the most, prankish boys would occasionally throw stones at him to provoke his verbal abuse. Then the boys would run away, laughing, when he pursued them. But almost everyone took him as a matter of course.

I neared the streetlight. Billy Graham's shirt, unbuttoned as usual, was pulled down on one side, revealing a naked shoulder. The shirt sleeve on that side hid his fingers and made it appear, from a distance, as though one hand was longer than the other. He placed the Bible on the small cane-seated upright mahogany chair, which he always brought out with him, and wiped the perspiration from his face with the bottom of his shirt.

'...And *you*,' he said, suddenly turning around and facing me, '...you is one o' those boys who threw stones at me last night?' I saw the twisted face, the froth at the corners of his mouth, the shoulder blades angled with dread. A sudden terror gripped me. Suddenly, this harmless character seemed menacing. I didn't even venture a reply but fled down the road clutching my father's lunch and sped up the tree-

47

mottled hill that led to Whitehall Main Road. Not once did I look behind me.

I gained the top of the hill. Winded, I set the lunch box on a large rock and crouched underneath the huge tamarind tree near it to regain my breath. The tree's leaves and branches were like large arms shading my fears. After a few minutes, I stood up, soaked with perspiration, and looked down to the Kings Road intersection. Light-grey smoke from someone's trash pile billowed from a yard. Then I saw him. Billy Graham sat in the mahogany chair, Bible clasped in front him, head held down deep. A praying mantis. A village prophet. God's horse.

I took up my father's lunch box and made my way along Whitehall Main Road until I came to the Nazarene Church. I stood by the bus pole in front of the church so that my father would be easily able to spot me. I loved to feel the warm breezes against my face and the shak-a-shakking of the dried pods of the flamboyant tree which guarded the church. Fallen petals formed a circular red carpet underneath the tree. Quarrelsome black birds darted in and out of the splayed branches.

I used to refer to the bus as 'my father's bus'. When it drew up and the automated door swung noisily open, pride like a fat ripened breadfruit swelled inside me. I got in and sat in the seat adjacent to the driver's, which my father always tried to reserve for me. This he would normally manage except on particularly busy days. Smiling, I handed him the lunch box and sat back. I enjoyed the long ride to the end of the route near a place called Holders Green. The bus soon approached my school, Montgomery Boys. As the bus got nearer, I focused my attention on the huge green eternity of a tamarind tree standing next to the school's low yard wall, and I tried to spot my favorite seat in the middle of the trunk. Boys fought furiously each day to acquire that coveted position: a U-shaped cutout near the top of the trunk that cradled one's body and gave the occupier a panoramic view of the playing field to the east, the school yard to the west, and, to the south, the dozens of corrugated roof-tops beneath the hill that shimmered like little zinc lakes. I once saw two dogs stuck together on the playing field and a man purposefully striding toward them with a water bucket in his hand. The moving bus didn't allow me to see the outcome of that confrontation, but I guessed what it was. In my own neighbourhood, similar sights were not uncommon.

About forty-five minutes later, the bus regained the Nazarene Church. I disembarked with a wave of the hand and my father's breeze-warm 'See you later, son' soothing my ears.

He was in control, guiding his bus effortlessly around each corner. He made it look so easy. And this casualness was compounded by his frequent horn-tooting, or his hand-waving, or his lusty 'hellos' directed toward people he recognized standing by corner shops or simply walking or driving along the burning asphalt. So where had it all gone wrong? Lying there on my bed, a discontented fifteen, I saw a powerless man, one at least who lacked the means to help me fit into the world I wanted and that appeared to want me: the world of my middle-class and wealthy peers.

I curl up with shame over my feelings towards these good, hard-working people who were dedicated to each other and to me. It was, for instance, during a lull in employment that my father decided to try his hand at the Farm Labor Program. It was also because, since being diagnosed with hypertension two years earlier, my mother's health had deteriorated, to the point where she was visibly slower in her gait. My father firmly suggested she stopped working all together. He said he would make enough money in Maryland to carry out repairs to the house. Through my mother, he had also been promised the job of chauffeur to old Mr. and Mrs. Simpson on his return from Maryland's corn and tobacco fields. With the expense of repairs taken care of, he would be able to support the entire family off his salary from the Simpsons. My mother agreed on condition that she continue working until I finished high school in three years. She stressed how important it was that they see me through. My father was deeply worried over her health, and he said so. She over-ruled his well-meaning protests, and the matter was settled.

And there was always Elroy, or rather his absence, eating away at the contentment that could have been mine if I'd properly appreciated the loving security of my parents' house. I feared my friends ever finding out, of being thought contaminated by some genetic connection; I feared losing friends and being shunned because of this. I was in a cave in which Elroy's shadow moved, whose entrance had been sealed against any outside penetration. Only my family knew about Elroy. He was my skeleton in a gouged novel. A secret cave. A secret tomb.

At school I wore my social mask with growing difficulty. To be middle-class there, lower-class at home, and, every-where, to be concealing the family secret, was boring a hole inside me. When my peers talked about their brothers, the idea of Elroy leapt into my brain, hanging over me, uncertain, strained, before, finally, effervescing into nothingness. It was a pelican that never took flight, that only milled around within its prescribed circumference. Dark bird. Rummaging bird.

I was unable to give voice to the wheelchair with the baby's fat cheeks. Everyone would laugh at me, say I was crazy. Was I crazy? I felt an intimacy with Elroy, but it was an attachment in which lay the impossibility of attachment. When I was first told of Elroy, I wanted desperately to see him. But, over the years, the deliberateness with which my parents never mentioned Elroy's name (except in their prayers) caused curiosity to be replaced with a vertiginous fear. When my father went to Maryland, the distance allowed me to ask about Elroy again. It was far easier to make these inquiries by letter rather than face to face. Elroy had become a cerebral figure, a heady spectre. Ghost brother. Ghost box. Something that, if revealed to anyone outside the family, could turn the world against me and spoil any chance of social achievement. The ghost clung to me like a spider. The burden of secrecy seeped into me and changed my position in relation to others. I was always one step back from them, making room for Elroy's ghost.

No wonder the mask crumbled and my grades declined. No wonder, one by one, I dropped out of the Drama and Spanish clubs, the soccer and track teams, the Literary and Debating Society.

I was making room for Elroy's ghost. The teachers said I had become withdrawn.

I heard the side door crack open. I instantly jumped off the bed, fished out a stick of jasmine incense and a box of matches from the top drawer of the mahogany chest of drawers, and lit the stick. I blew hard on the end of it so that it glowed like an ember. When I stopped blowing, the smoke billowed thickly and then settled into a slow elegant spiral in the shape of the number '8'. Like a priest with his censer, I waved the smoking incense around the room.

'Alph?' my mother called. Her footsteps were heavy on the pine floors. I shouted to her that I was in my room. Shortly, the bedroom door opened, and she appeared. She was heavily-built, in her early fifties. Her imposing figure contrasted with her soft, round, almost girlish face. She wore a blue head-tie and a cream uniform. Pressed hair. A black wave rolled from underneath the head-tie across her forehead.

'Wha' that smell so in here, Alphonso?' She screwed her

brows tightly, then looked around the room with furtive glances.

'Just some incense, Mum,' I said, 'to freshen up the room.' I lay on the bed and turned onto my right side to address her. She eyed me with a puzzled expression.

'I hope that is what it is,' she said. 'You hearing a lot 'bout this dope and everything nowadays. Your father and I learn a lot from watching that TV in there. You be careful, hear me?'

'All right, Mum.'

'You ate the food I left in the fridge for you?'

'Yeah.'

'Good. De devil roaming up and down the earth, hear? Left and right. Mind how you go.'

She turned and left me, and I rolled on to my other side hearing the clatter of pots and pans echoing from the kitchen. I got up, took the Marley off the turntable, put on a Sparrow LP, and lay back down. Suddenly, I hopped off the bed as if I were fleeing some approaching dread which only I could see. The music seized me, and I began gyrating to the calypso rhythms. I flailed my arms and hands, driving back the invisible demons. I worked myself into a perspiring frenzy and then rolled on to the bed again, exhausted, a little relieved.

The next day my father was expected home from Maryland. I got home around six o'clock, just as the sun had started to sink below the horizon. I came through the side door, and his eyes instantly caught mine. He and my mother sat at the dining table over enamel plates of rice and beef stew.

'Hello, Son,' he said, raising his chin and smiling broadly.

'Hi, Dad,' I said going over to him. He pushed the wrought iron chair back and stood up to hug me. My mother said, 'The food just heat-up, Alph. Go and help you'self.'

As I was turning to go, I saw my father glance through the

top glass pane of the side door. For a brief moment I saw, with him, the surround of the sun's pink and orange glow, the swarms of bats darting in and out of the darkening mango, breadfruit, and coconut trees. They dove or shot up from the utility wires as if fleeing some terror they'd sensed but could not see. When I returned to the table, he was shaking his head. I didn't know if this was in response to something my mother had said or in response to what I felt was a momentary omen he and I had just witnessed.

'It wasn't bad, you know,' he said, looking at my mother again. 'It did hard work all right (but I used to hard work anyways, right?). And the pay did good. I didn't mix up too much wid the other men, but I got along well with all of them anyways.'

'Well, you did the best thing,' she said. 'You doan mix-up you'self with everybody, 'specially when you got work to do. You wus there to work and come back home to you family. We glad enough you back. Sometimes, I did worried sick when we get all the news 'bout the violence out there, you hear?'

My father sucked on a salted pig's tail with the air of a somnambulist. Whatever dish was prepared, he insisted on an accompanying salt-meat bone, as they called it. As night fell, he got up to turn on the light. He stood about five feet six inches tall, brown-skinned, some grey at the temples, crew cut hair parted on the left side. His feet were like hands lightly slapping the floor boards, and this action caused his waist to jerk rhythmically when he walked.

'How things going, Son? How's school?' he asked, on his way back to the table and the pig's tail.

'Good,' I said.

'He all right,' my mother added. 'He just a little distracted like I told you in my last letter. He got "O" levels this coming June. I really hope he pull heself up and mek de grade.'

'I believe he will, E. We got to believe that. If I had de oppurtunities like he... man, I tell you, I woulda been a doctor or lawyer or somebody big today.'

'You ain' lie. I know you would be. But, Alph, why you coming in later and later? And what is that funny smell I notice coming from you room?'

'Is just incense, Mum,' I said, 'to freshen the room.'

'Well, E. You know, you can't be too hard on him, you know. After all, he's a boy child, and he mus' have his friends and his freedom.'

'I hope he pick the right ones. My father and mother always used to tell me to pick and choose your friends, 'cause some of them can lead you astray real bad, you hear?'

After dinner and my father's regular compliment to my mother ('E? My gut is well-charged'), the couple went into the living room to watch *Days of Our Lives* and the local news. I continued eating at the table from where I could see them through the archway separating the rooms. He opened the windows wider to allow the cool night breezes uninhibited entry. The streetlight, two houses down from ours, would be glowing outward in a circumference of about forty yards and then everything, the straggly khus-khus hedges, the pot-holed asphalt, other houses with their neatly-trimmed hedges, eddied into pitch blackness. A band of whistling frogs were now in their sixth or seventh set.

When the news program finished, my father switched off the television set and repeated to my mother how happy he was that the US dollars would not only repair the house but also pay off the land loan and transform the wooden kitchen and rear bedroom into brick.

'When I start with the Simpsons, I goin' be a free man,' he said. He tilted his head back and smiled, and he smacked his lips as he did when feeding on a salt-meat bone.

'And E? The next thing I want to do is get a lil' second-hand car. A lil' station wagon or something. I could even sell some greens on the side: carrots, peppers, lettuce, cabbage, that sort o' thing. What you think, E?'

'I know you like you kitchen gardening, and I doan see why not. But I doan know if you'll have the time or the energy to do all that, Fitz. Everybody know what a slave-driver Mrs. Simpson is.'

'Who? The old girl? She don' frighten me, man.' He laughed loudly, but it was dryish.

'Well, but she could be a mean one. She is the kinda woman that does call on you any time – day or night – and expect you to come running. Mr. Simpson have a heart in he chest, but Mrs. Simpson? Let me tell yuh. She is a real old-time white woman, you hear? A real old-time white woman.'

'She don' frighten me.'

'You got to use big brain on her. I survived her for fifteen years. Fifteen years. Once you get the children and grands to like you, you'll survive the old woman. There ain't nothing to she like she offspring and blood. I doan like to throw blame, but she is part o' de reason I got this pressure now. As I say, old Mr. Simpson is all right, and them ain' the worse White people out. But you got to watch the old woman. Mek sure she doan work you into a early grave, you hear?'

'I won' let her do that. I'd throw 'way the job first before I let that happen. How's the other boy?'

'Same way. No ways worse. I went and look for him last Saturday as usual. He's in God's hands.'

'Yes. Alphonso keep asking about him ev'ry time he write me.'

'Well, I guess Alph at the age where he could use a big brother. He want a big brother to look up to. But if he see he brother in the condition that he in, it would only break his heart and mek he life a lot worse off. He doan need to see him like that.'

'That's what I told him. Is hard even for we who bring

55

him into this world,' my father said, and got up to turn the T.V. on again. I rose from the table and told them I was going down by one of my friends for a while.

I came home around ten-thirty. The side door had been left open for me. I pulled the door and stepped over Tiger Man, my gray cat, spotted black with a few white stripes near his neck. I stepped too far over him and banged yet again into one of the wrought iron dining room chairs. The chair fell to the ground with a loud thud.

'Wha' all that noise?' I heard my father ask as I limped toward the bathroom.

'Alph?' My mother's voice. Inside the bathroom, my right hand made a practised glide up the wall and flicked on the light switch. Immediately, as the shock of light fell, a giant bubble of aquamarine enfolded me. I only realized that it was the colour of the bathroom walls when I heard my father's mixed-breed dog, Bronze, howling in the back yard. Bronze was part German Shepherd and part Labrador, named for his colour. Early every morning, before breakfast, my father took him for a walk through the neighbourhood, allowing him to defecate at will in the hedges of khus-khus grass. From time to time, there would be complaints from neighbours about the dog's indiscriminate easing of its bowels on someone's property or about Bronze's tendency to bare his teeth and growl at any and every one. My father bought bone meal from the supermarket each week. Bronze's Sunday meal. During the rest of the week, he would be fed our leftovers and the generous leftovers of the Simpsons.

I urinated and flushed the toilet bowl, returned to pick up the fallen chair, and, with heavy, uncoordinated steps, presented myself under the archway which separated the living and dining rooms.

'Hey, Dad,' I said.

56

'Hi, Son.'

We looked at each other, and an ancient awkwardness elbowed its way between us. It made my father shift around in the caned mahogany Morris chair in which he sat. It made me try to rub the marijuana from my face. It made my father turn one eye to the safety of the television set. But even if I could have redirected his eye in my direction, I wouldn't have done so. I wouldn't have risked exposing my residual stupor by inviting closer scrutiny. So I just stood there watching him watch the T.V. with one eye and me with the other. My mother, still brimming with the satisfaction of having us all together again, rocked gently in the mahogany rocking chair in the right corner of the room. During the television advertisements, she hummed Anglican hymns.

My father expressed himself much better in writing. The communication gap between us had temporarily ceased with the letters, but now, like some latent sore, it surfaced again. I wanted things to be different between us, and I knew he wanted this as well. But, somewhere along the way, my father's all-powerful image had been killed off, and this robbed me of the paternal inspiration I sought. It seemed as if he no longer understood my needs. Before high school, this wasn't the case, but my exposure to secondary education opened the dream of another life, a life free of embarrassing village characters, a life in which one's father drove one to school in a white Peugeot. We had accomplished the first part of that quest by leaving Kings Road. It seemed as though the second part would never be accomplished. A second-hand station wagon, from which vegetables would be sold, was not quite the same.

Suddenly, I felt a great need to get away, to flee from him, so I headed toward the kitchen, my movements swift yet uncertain. I sensed that my parents had realized I wasn't acting normally, but that they didn't know how to approach me on the subject. This might have been part of my father's earlier awkwardness as well. I opened the door of the refrigerator, took out some leftover rice and stew, and lumbered back to the dining table. I set the bowl down before me and spooned up the food in a steady rhythm.

'That food want warming, Alph,' I heard my mother say. I didn't think so. I crammed it down. I could not see her from through the archway, but my father was in full view. I saw him get up, heard the TV turned off, and saw him return to his seat. It was then I resigned myself to my fate.

'How were things in Maryland?' I asked, straining to sound and act normal. He swung his stretched-out feet from off the worn brown ottoman. Some silent communication, it seemed, was going on between my parents, because, at the same time he responded to my question with his feet, my mother walked past him and turned on the living room light. She must have sensed that her husband and son were trying to be friends, were trying to reach out to each other, and she would do whatever she could (however oblique, however understated) to facilitate this. After she had returned to the rocking chair and was satisfied that the setting for the gulf-crossing had been established, she got up and walked past my father again. This time, she disappeared into the bedroom leaving my father and me alone.

He looked just as he had always looked prior to his Maryland trip. Same thick moustache flecked with grey. Same wavy hair streaked with grey and parted on the left side. Same loud voice.

'All right, Son – in the name of the Lord,' he said and sneezed. Same loud sneeze that, it was said, could be heard eight houses down the road. He flopped his feet on top of the ottoman again. I put the fork into the empty bowl, got up and sat in the *Morris* chair adjacent to him.

'You set for you "O" levels?' he asked, when I had settled in my seat.

'Pretty much.' The stupor had more or less left me. My

coordination was returning. I smiled inwardly, pleasantly surprised by the conversational ease between us.

'Good, good. Just put God first and you'll do well at whatsoever you put your hands on. Meditate on Joshua One, my favourite *script*—ture.' His feet swung off the ottoman, and he sat up straight. 'Yes, my Son. For success, nothing can beat that *scrip*—ture.' He repeated the word *scripture* with what seemed like relishing emphasis, a stress on the first syllable, followed by a lengthy pause, and then a softer second syllable. Trochaic metre, my English teacher Miss Gamble would have said. It was as if my father had suddenly made some marvellous phonetic discovery.

'Ah, *Scrip*—ture!' he said again. 'Nothing can beat it, my Son. 'Tis what keep me and your mother going all these years.'

I was beginning to feel uncomfortable again. Everything had been going so well a moment ago. Now, I felt myself bracing for a lengthy sermon on my father's personal history – which I had heard so many times before. Often, I have to admit, I felt intense irritation, revulsion even, listening to it. It wasn't until I had left the island, and when it was too late, that I understood his lamentations to be cathartic. He was purging himself of the horrors of his upbringing to make his own salvation possible. The fear and trembling invoked by the tragic circumstances of his early life purified him and allowed the Word, the Scripture, to quicken his dead past, his pre-Elvina past. He had, in fact, achieved some measure of happiness in this life. More than happiness. Contentment. But now, his lengthy lectures about his misfortunes and about God, seemed both remote and very present – like Elroy. Very present. Very elusive. Ghost lectures. All over my life hung one cloud, one ghost, or another. How could I escape?

I told him I felt tired and that I was going to bed. He must

59

have felt the same way because, as soon as I walked away, I heard him get up and walk towards the bedroom.

In the cocoon of my room, I turned on the light and lay flat on my back. I thought about the group of musicians with whom I had teamed up over the past few weeks and the good times we had. I played rhythm guitar with the group. We all went to different high schools (all, except the drummer Ian who was a high-school dropout). We had met liming on Friday evenings at the bus terminal. It had begun one Friday when Mr. Riley was unable to pick up Christopher and me. I liked the liming, so I continued with it. By the time I had finished Fourth Form, I ceased riding with Christopher altogether, preferring the company of my new friends. As for Ian being a dropout, this gave him a certain glamour in our eyes – as did the fact that, although he didn't have a job, he always had lots of money. Later, we found out that he had a girlfriend in the U.S. who sent him money each month. He was an excellent drummer, smart and charming, so he fulfilled our criteria.

It had taken me only six months to master the rhythm guitar. I made a fret board out of a strip of card eight inches long, drew on the strings and frets, and wrote on the names of each note, and then I covered it all with strips of transparent tape. During the Spanish, History, and French classes (my worst subjects), I held the miniature fingerboard in front of my desk, moving my fingers all over it and memorizing the notes. If a teacher noticed my distraction, I'd put the finger-board on my knee and raise the knee on to the underside of the desk. I saved every penny from my allowance and, after a couple of months of admiring an Edmond in Mannings' Showroom each evening on my way home from school, I bought my first acoustic guitar for forty dollars.

The Ordinary Level exams temporarily aborted my involvement with the group, but I found relaxation and pleasure in playing the guitar and got into the habit of playing for an hour or so before and after finishing my homework. Indeed, this pleasure took my mind off my preoccupation with Elroy – and my anger with my parents. They were happy with my new mood. The exam results came in one day in July: seven out of eight passes. Failed History. Scraped a pass in French, but, surprisingly, passed Spanish with a B grade. Distinctions in Physics, Chemistry, and Maths. Parental jubilation.

'Thank you Jesus!' my mother cried on receiving the news. 'I just know you would mek the grade, Alph.'

My father said, 'Well done, Son. If I had the oppurtunities like you, I'd be a doctor or a lawyer or somebody big today.'

'Yuh know yuh right,' my mother said.

I remember those mid-summers, how they came like an armed man, sudden and violent, the sun's shimmering lake of silver flooding everything. I see myself getting off the bus in Fairchild Street and heading across the bridge towards Broad Street, happily conscious of the black case in my right hand which contained the object of my affections. On the outside of the guitar case, a colourful Bob Marley, hair flying outward like the leafy branches of a tree, sang and danced from a circular sticker. I gazed over to the Chamberlain Bridge and then to the fishing boats in the Careenage's dark, murky water. Tourists entered and exited the gift shops and restaurants that lined the far side of the waterfront. A mulatto man briskly unwound the rope which moored a medium-sized fibreglass yacht. A small group of tourists stood on its deck, supporting themselves on to the deck rails. A tug, belonging to the Harbour Police, gouged a furrow as it chugged out to sea. At the head of this street, where the grim statue of Admiral Lord Nelson towered in bronze, I stopped to buy a coconut-flavoured sno-cone from a vendor, and then continued walking southward in the direction of the Lower Green bus terminal.

In ten minutes, I was at the terminal but changed my mind about taking a bus to Mike's house in Fontabelle. I continued walking, going past Cheapside and its poorly maintained vegetable markets, past the Fleet Street of Barbados's newspaper industry, the balustraded, porched and pillared older houses, and industrial brick buildings housing Hanshell Inniss Distributors of Fine Spirits and other warehouses. Then I made a right turn on to Woodville Avenue and was soon opening the high wrought-iron gate to Mike's house.

Having long finished the sno-cone, streams of perspiration were running down my back and the insides of my arms. My shirt was sticking to my body like another layer of skin. I climbed the front steps of the house and, for a few minutes, stood in the comforting shade of the trellised porch, admiring the vines of yellow bell-shaped flowers crawling through the trellis work. I pressed the doorbell. On this Friday afternoon, the neighbourhood, save for some moderate traffic, stood motionless, imprisoned in heat. I rung the doorbell again and, in a few seconds, Mike opened the door.

Mike was the bass player in our group, *The Cream of Sweets*. The idea for the group's name had sprung on us one Saturday morning at Mike's home when the group's organist, Lee, discovered a Cream of Wheat cereal carton on top of Mike's bass amp. After we'd all given him a hard time ('Baby has to get his cereal'; 'Poor baby, the cereal box empty'; 'O, don't cry, baby. Mummy'll get you some more'), Ian, the drummer, suggested we call the group *The Cream of Sweets*. There was unanimous agreement.

'Where's Mrs. Thompson?' I asked as we walked through the house to his room at the back. I heard faint drum sounds and guitar riffs which got louder and louder as we approached. I couldn't wait to join them.

'Oh, she came in already, but she went back out,' he said. Mike, at least six feet tall, walked with his right shoulder perpetually raised as if he were constantly playing his bass. His body stood strangely erect while, simultaneously, it seemed, leaning to the left in a curious diagonal. Inside his room, partially soundproofed with egg boxes and littered with music magazines, I plugged in my Edmond (to which I had attached a micro-pickup), and tuned it to Steve's second-hand Fender. Dimpled Steve. Freckled Steve. Fair-skinned Steve with the flat buttocks and the clear snaky brown eyes. After tuning up, we began a reggae jam. Mike played like he walked, rocking sideways to the point of falling over and then, as if with a sudden change of heart, straightening up again.

The doorbell rang again. Mike went to answer it; the rest of us kept on playing. He soon returned with the organist, Lee, a short perpetually-smiling fifteen-year-old with a smooth, round, girl-like face and a line for a mouth. Mike took up his guitar again, and Lee switched on his organ to join the jam session. Ian flashed his long brown dreadlocks from side to side. Occasionally, Lee would stop playing the keyboards and take the tambourine from the top of the organ, and bang it on the outside of his right knee. Whenever the music was in perfect harmony, we'd all simultaneously look at each other and smile or grin or shout, 'Yeah!!'

Around six o'clock we took a break. Some of us sat on Mike's bunk bed, others sat on the floor or an old couch. Mike's stereo boomed with some of our own music recently recorded on a domestic cassette player. He took out a plastic bag with some spliffs from inside a pouch he kept in the wardrobe, and we lit up. The doorbell rang once more. I thought it was Mike's mother. To tell you the truth, I was very attracted to her. She was always fashionably dressed. Slim, youthful body. Angular features. Dimpled cheeks. She probably was in her early forties and taught at a Montessori school. She and Mike's father had divorced three years ago; Mike's elder brother and sister had already left home. A knock sounded on the bedroom door, followed by a female voice which, because of the loudness of the music, I was unable to identify.

'Come in!' shouted Mike, who was the closest to the door. When he said that, I knew then it couldn't have been his mother. Jackee and Cicely entered the room, laughing and joking with each other. They were both making out with Steve, although, officially, Cicely was Steve's woman. Jackee, fair-skinned, shortish, voluptuous figure; Cicely, caramel, very slender.

'Hi, fellas,' Cicely said. 'Look like we come just in time.' She gyrated through the smoky room like a vertical snake, snake body wriggling and jerking suggestively with each step she took. Snake body drawn to snake eyes. She went over to the couch, on which Steve was lying, and sat pertly on him. He put his spliff between her thick red lips, lips that seemed to glow even more when they were around the burning butt. Jackee flirted with Mike. From his pocket, he took out a phial which contained some little pellets, put two in his mouth and one in Jackee's. They washed them down with coke, and the phial was passed to Steve, Cicely, Ian, Lee and, finally, me.

My apprehension had already been growing when I first saw the phial sliding in my direction. As it got closer to me, I increasingly felt stifled, choked. My mother's words seized my throat. *Mind how you go*. I had heard of the addictive quality of such drugs and had no desire or intention to trespass on that ground.

'What are they?' I asked when the phial reached me.

'Pelicans in flight,' Mike said. 'Otherwise known as acid.' He laughed and hugged Jackee. Half of me fled through the door. The other half, weakened by the marijuana, held on to the people in the room and clung to that common soil. It wasn't long before my apprehension vanished like a ghost, and I joined the ritual of my peers.

Later that night, asleep in my own room, I dreamt I was in an apartment with Mike's mother and my Spanish teacher Mr. Phillips. I had just acquired a hand gun and was discussing its features with Mr. Phillips when someone knocked on the door. I placed the gun in a nearby drawer and looked through the peep hole. A man, side-turned, was standing there. The man had a familiar aura. I opened the door, and the man turned to face me. The man was me! Mike's mother shrieked and huddled behind Mr. Phillips. I saw a gun in my twin's hand and raced over to the drawer for mine. Twin raised his weapon, and I was forced to shoot him in the foot, hoping he'd stop his insanity. But he returned fire and caught me in the abdomen. The force of his bullet knocked me backward to the floor. Vision diminishing, I looked up at Twin in disbelief and saw the flesh fall off of him in huge chunks. The teeth and jaw bones of the skeleton clattered, 'Got yuh!'

I awoke with a start and a deep raking groan. The strangest feeling swept over me. I felt as if something was drawing me away from this world, drawing my mind but not my body. This separation of mind and body made me feel that I was no longer who I was, that I was someone else looking at me. Yet, I felt a bond, some curious alliance with the other person who was looking at me now from across the room. Was it a ghost brother? A ghost self? This loss of control over who I was triggered a lancing fear that made my heart shudder helplessly and hot and cold currents run under my skin. I rushed to the bathroom, switched on the light, and looked into the plastic-framed mirror over the wash basin. A face, blurry at first, swam into view. It was Elroy's. I saw the unmistakable fat cheeks. He was not smiling. His face carried both sorrow and rage. What had I done to anger him so? Who was he sorrowing for? Me? Himself? What could I do to ease his ancient grief? He wore an old, worn, brown felt hat and a tweed jacket which was rifled with holes and patches. A black and grey moustache. His face rivered with wrinkles. Several times I looked down at myself and then into the mirror at the homeless Elroy. Barefooted, the derelict went outside and stumbled down the street. We both felt cut off from the world. Out on Redman's Main Road, at this midnight hour, I increasingly felt a need to throw myself in front of the passing traffic. Some force outside me (was it Elroy?) urged me in wheedling tones to do so, and my will buckled and sagged.

I felt metal slam into me like a giant fist trying to punch me out of existence. I folded in half amid the frenzied screech of tyres. The blow lifted me on to the car's bonnet and up on to the windshield. For a second, I glimpsed the driver's numbed face. My own shocked bowels gave way, and I rolled off the bonnet and struck the warm asphalt. Everything went black.

The circumstances surrounding the accident were somewhat blurred, I would eventually find out from my father. The driver of the car wasn't too clear on what had happened or who was at fault. There had been no eye witnesses. But my parents wanted to know why I was dressed in an old jacket and felt hat, was walking the streets barefooted, and why I had used black shoe polish and white liquid paper to paint on my face a moustache and black tributaries of wrinkles.

My father's first cousin, Aunt Lolita (the only family member who had married into wealth), had two sons, one of whom was a medical practitioner. So my father consulted with Ronald who, after visiting me a week or so after I'd regained consciousness, concluded that my psychological condition was of greater concern than my physical wounds. The accident was the culmination of some deeper problem. It was a mask, he said, a facade over the real issues. Ronald must have advised my father to seek the help of a psychologist, Letitia Archer, for she replaced Ronald as my counsellor. Twice a week, she visited me at the hospital.

'Why were you dressed the way you were on the night of the accident, Alphonso? Your parents (who love you very much) want to know.'

'Dressed like what?' She told me. I said I couldn't remember. I was with my friends making music, had got home around eleven-thirty. After that, I remembered nothing until I woke up in a hospital ward.

'Do your friends take drugs?' she asked, her eyes wide, brown lakes of sympathy. I said nothing.

'You must tell me, Alphonso. It's the only way to begin to make you better. Tell me what it was you took.' I refused to say anything more to her and sat like a stone as she continued trying, unsuccessfully, to get me to open up. Later, I realized that she must have already known what I'd taken, because she would have been given access to my hospital records.

Her time with me expired, and she rose to go. As she neared the ward's exit, Dr. Archer suddenly turned around and looked at my expressionless body sitting in the chair next to the bed. She then walked back to me, crouched, and kissed me on the cheek. I saw invisible tears run down her cheeks.

For two weeks I continued to refuse to respond to her questions about drugs. I was more afraid of my parents finding out than I was of letting Dr. Archer know. My mother had been suspicious for some time. I recalled her scepticism over the jasmine incense which I burned in my room from time to time. The thought of her and my father knowing the truth about my habits bolted the door on disclosure. My secret was burning a hole inside me though, and I felt lonelier than ever during those days. I hoped Dr. Archer would hug me. How I hoped she would embrace me. More and more, I sensed Dr. Archer carried the secret of my relief. She became the logical choice, since none of my friends ever visited. Her sad brown eyes wept for me on each visitation, eyes that contained all my silent suffering, eyes that calmly drained my fears. She had strength in those almond-dreamy eyes. Her kiss on my cheek (along with her carnival-coloured outfits) became a ritual of expectation each time she visited. One day, I confessed everything to her and the ensuing feeling was as if a giant sea rock had been lifted off me, letting me float back up to the surface.

During my final weeks in hospital, I started playing my guitar again. At first, I had sworn I wouldn't touch another guitar as long as I lived, but Dr. Archer somehow managed to convince me that music was a part of who I was and that I should be kinder to myself.

'You're associating your music with the bad experience you had, because they were happening at the same time. And that's normal. But they're quite separate. Hold on to the beauty of your music, Alphonso. The beauty of yourself.'

So I asked her if she would collect my guitar and bring it the next time she came to see me. Eventually, I started playing for the residents of my ward, folk songs and even a few hymns whose melodies and lyrics I still remembered from Sunday School. Bringing cheer to others in this manner, lifted my own spirit and took me out of myself. I regularly sauntered around the wards and the corridors on my floor, chatting to the nurses and whoever else I encountered. I liked going over to the paediatric unit where something always seemed to be going on: clowns, folk musicians and, one day in early August, a magician.

I stood inside the ward, near the doorway, watching the caped, smiling figure and the popping eyes of the young audience. I heard frequent gasps punctuate the room like cresting waves.

'How you did that, man?' I asked the Indo-Caribbean illusionist afterwards. I was referring to the last act in which he made pennies go from one hand to the other. The magician smiled and smiled, wrapped in a blue velvet suit with a velvet cape that was blue on the outside and red underneath. He didn't reply.

'You made those coins go from one hand to the other at will, man. I was watching you real close, man. How on earth you did that?'

'It's magic,' he replied. His glossy black moustache quivered on top of his smile. Later, he told me he was from Couva, in Trinidad, was a high school teacher, and was in the island for an Education seminar. Magic was his passion outside the classroom. He said he hoped one day to be able to go to the United States to really develop his magical skills.

'Yeah, but I'm an intelligent man,' I pressed. 'I followed your every move and still couldn't get it. What *did* you do?'

'Magicians never tell their secrets,' he replied, 'but this much I'll tell you. You have to practice to be natural. The eyes only see. The brain tells you *what* to see. If you can control the brain through magic, through illusion, you'll therefore see only what the brain dictates for you to see. But the illusion must mimic nature, must be based on natural things like sea breezes, rivers, caves, trees. Things that are pure, uncorrupted. I strive to be natural with my magic. If my brain interprets a movement as stilted, then my confidence sags and the magic fails. If, on the other hand, my brain perceives the movements as natural, it becomes so and, through incessant practice, my illusion (which is my reality) works. It's what they call suspension of disbelief. It's a fiction, but real truth is achieved through illusion. It's mind over matter, really.'

I was borne away on the tide of his self-assurance; I wanted to inhabit his world and envied his energy.

'And you have to trust the illusion, right? I mean, you musn't fear it.'

'You got it,' Couva Magician nodded, smiling his knowing smile.

69

'And so,' I said, 'however a man thinks is how he is, right?'

'Precisely.'

'I get the point.'

After my discharge, the sessions with Dr. Archer continued for most of the remainder of summer. She seemed delighted with the speed of my recovery. I visited her office in Belleville twice a week at first, then once a week. My father could ill afford the fees, but Dr. Archer was considerate.

'Thanks for thanking me, Alphonso,' she said, 'but don't worry about it. Your father and I will work something out. He's a good man, you know. And he really cares about you.'

'Well, thanks again, Dr. Archer. And if you need someone to make your coffee, sweep floors, do anything, just let me know.' We laughed together and, for the first time, I saw her as a woman: how full and even were her lips that spread across pearly teeth. Then, with a look that indicated how proud she was of me, she reached out and hugged me at last.

'Do you strive to be natural, Dr. Archer?' I couldn't get out of my mind what Couva Magician had said. *Practice to be natural.*

'What do you mean?' she asked and brought her hand to rest loosely on my shoulders. I paraphrased my conversation with the magician. She drew a contrast between the awed, happy children under the influence of natural illusion (smiling Couva illusionist) and my running fear and depression under the influence of unnatural illusion (drugs). She said the risks and the dangers of taking drugs were not worth it.

'Keep making your music, Alphonso,' she admonished with a soft sigh. 'Happy music.'

The shock I received as a result of the nightmare trip made me feel that drugs, in any form, were unnatural, and my revulsion became almost religious. The first thing I did when I got home was to systematically remove all the posters from my bedroom walls. I didn't call any of my friends, for not once had any of them visited me. This bothered me a great deal. It was the way we Barbadians were about anyone with psychological problems. Madness was contagious. Even when sanity was restored, the social stigma remained. Lying on my back in bed, I concluded that those friendships were part of an unnatural illusion.

I tried very hard to focus on my school work. It wasn't easy. I'd have a great desire to see my old friends again. Once, I even dialled Steve's number, but hearing my old friend's voice, I hung up the phone without replying. I cleaved to my guitar as if it were a person. I called her Acoustic Woman. I preferred her company.

Once, a girl from the neighbourhood, who went to St. Michael's school and with whom I'd talk at the bus stand, stopped by to see me one April evening after school. I heard a knock on the front door and opened the front window out to her.

'I went to the shop and thought I'd stop by and say hello,' she said. She was around sixteen, very dark-skinned, very slender, dimpled, with the whitest teeth I'd ever seen. White T-shirt and blue jeans. She shifted her weight from one foot to the other in a stationary dance.

'Hi,' I said after overcoming my initial surprise. My guitar had been my girlfriend all year, and now it was difficult to include anyone else. What else was I to say to her but 'hi'? Try as I might, no other words would allow themselves to be formed. An awkward feeling swept over me, and I felt defeated, unable or unwilling to connect to her. The more she stood there with her toothy smiles and flirtatious stationary dance, the more I wanted to be alone with my guitar.

'Well, I gotta be going,' she finally said. 'See yuh.'

I fled back into my room to my guitar. I took it out of its plastic case and sat on the edge of the bed. When I raised my right arm to play, I felt rivers of sweat running down my arms and sides.

A year later, I passed Advanced Level Maths, Physics, and Chemistry with A grades and, for nine months afterwards (while working as a clerk in the Library Service), I played solo guitar professionally. By then, I'd grown more comfortable with flesh and blood women. This had been achieved largely through Clarence Browne's coaching and the many opportunities for relationships which opened to me as a musician. Years later, I would remind Clarence that he taught me all I knew about women.

But pleasant as this life was, I felt restless. I felt that I had to get out of the island or be doomed, at best to a mundane career as a civil servant. My parents were not white, wealthy, members of any political party or other influential organizations. They had no strings to pull. Also, there were people outside my family who knew that I had briefly undergone psychological counselling. Suppose that secret were to escape and gyrate maliciously over the island, spoiling my chances of success? I had to get away. I had to flee the spectre of shame that danced in circles around me. My performance in the Advanced Level exams earned me a scholarship to Louisiana State University to pursue a bachelor of science degree in Engineering. I did well as an undergraduate. Straight A's. Dean's list. Cum Laude graduate.

CHAPTER FIVE

Simone called upstairs to say that after she had checked the girls she would come up to help me pack. I put the letter and book out of sight. When she arrived we packed quietly but companionably for some time. The phone rang. It was evidently her mother whose telephone calls of late had increased like sorrow. Probably wanted to check that I was on my way. It was after Simone's visit to her mother in Louisiana, now about three months ago, that she'd returned even more decided about separating from me than before she'd left. I wasn't at all surprised.

Today, though, the call was unusually brief.

'Don't want me to be dogged out by your mother today, Simone?' I said when she called me downstairs for a cup of tea and a break from packing. She didn't reply. I said, 'What happen? She run out of bad jokes about Caribbean men who joke too much and smile all the time?'

'Maybe I should've heeded her warnings.'

We were referring to what we had termed 'The Uncle Samuel' jokes. Mrs. Williams had a friend whose mother was born in Barbados, who often told her stories of doggish uncles. Simone would say her mother meant well in sharing such stories, had her interest at heart; she herself didn't place any value in such hand-me-down stories. But Simone's suggestions of hyperbole and untruthful garnishing were never enough to prevent her mother from recounting such tales nor believing in their veracity.

One such tale, I recalled Simone telling me, centred around a certain Uncle Samuel who lived in Brooklyn, who allegedly had harems of women both in America and in Barbados. One day, Samuel left one of his American women's homes en route to the airport for Barbados and another woman. On his way to the airport, he apparently lost control of the car. It ran off the road, flipped several times, and killed Uncle Samuel on the spot. No one knew which of his female friends to contact. Eventually, about six different women showed up at the morgue to identify and claim the body. Uncle Samuel used to smile a lot, my mother said. He was a real sweet-talker.

All this was unquestionably trivial, but it got to me more than it should have. It was one of the reasons why Simone sometimes felt uncomfortable with her mother and had both looked forward to and dreaded her visits. She knew that negative innuendos about me would flap from her mother like shawls of mistrust to wrap tightly around her daughter's shoulders. Although she respected her mother's opinions, there had been a time when I knew Simone would not have conspired in any way to disrespect me. But now it seemed that her opinion of me was firmly fixed. If I was honest, further pressure on her mother's part was now probably unnecessary. There must have come a point when Simone's defence of me against her mother must have seemed to her misplaced love, misplaced loyalty. Perhaps for some time she had suspected her mother was right about me, but her pride wouldn't let her admit any error in judgment. To condemn me would have been to admit her own blindness. Now her very fixed decision not to move with me seemed to me to concede to everything her mother had said.

'Your mother must be real happy,' I said.

'Sometimes ending things is necessary for growth. This relationship has really hurt me, Alphonso. I ain't gonna lie. But I feel liberated now. I sense great things coming.'

'Good for you,' I said. 'Good for you.'

'I'm concerned for the kids,' Simone said. 'It's the kids I worry about.'

'I know.'

'My mother once asked me what kind of man wants to shuttle from house to house instead of owning one? Come to think of it, Alphonso, I really don't know much about your family, your past, do I? After all this time. Of course, it's a little late for all that now, huh?'

'What more can I say, Simone? I was an only child. Both my parents died in a car accident. You know that. You were the first person I told.'

'Yes, you told me,' Simone said, shrugging her shoulders. 'That's sad. But what else didn't you tell me? Maybe you inherited this restlessness, huh?'

'*That* I also said was possible, Simone. My father. He changed residences a lot when I was young. Maybe that has something to do with it.'

'There must be more that you haven't told me. There has to be.'

I didn't reply. I went upstairs to resume packing.

This time, though my book beckoned, it was thinking about my relationship with Simone that kept me from making serious progress with my task. Although she had conceded serious marital problems to her mother, Simone, I knew, wasn't ready for divorce. Although she wanted to separate, she'd told me she dared not utter the word 'divorce' to her mother. That would have encouraged her too much, she'd said. Her mother would probably have volunteered to accompany Simone to the lawyer and to pay all the fees. I was sure Simone realized her decision not to move with me made divorce a strong possibility, perhaps even an inevitability, but I sensed that right now she wasn't ready for that.

She told me that once, while she was at college, her parents had almost divorced. They'd actually separated and, for several weeks her mother had stayed with her elder sister, Chantel. Chantel and Simone eventually had convinced their mother to return home. Why had she left? Her father was allegedly having an affair. It was quite certain he had done so before. Simone's half brother was evidence enough. This, I knew, was another reason why Simone hadn't wanted to open up the issue of divorce with her mother.

I was sure, though, that her mother's views were based on more than just maternal concern. Her attitude, I felt, was coloured by her own marital problems and her fear of Simone having to suffer a similar fate. All mothers wanted their daughters to fare better than they had done. It also seemed that Mama Williams had never forgiven me for moving her darling grandchildren so far away from Louisiana – or me out of reach of her hawkish observation. For hawkish observation it was. I'd left Louisiana genuinely for career reasons; the distance from Mrs. Williams's insistent picking on me was an inadvertent relief. Even Simone felt so. She'd tried to soothe her mother by telling her how much she appreciated the way she'd raised her, but this evidently did not convince Mama Williams. If she'd been as successful as her daughter claimed, how come the said daughter had chosen to marry a man who fell so far short of being proper and trustworthy?

Would things have gone better if I'd told Simone more about my troubled past? Had taken her to Barbados on holidays? Possibly. But she had given her mother only what information she had received from me. And so, she'd found it more and more difficult to justify my defence.

Simone understood the parts of me that I revealed. She never mistook my pride for arrogance, as other people had done. She rightly understood it to be a cultural pride. I still wrote and sung calypsos in my spare time. I still had a very healthy collection of steel pan, calypso, and reggae albums. But was I too proud? Had pride crossed the line to the point of being pathologically scornful? And what of my perfectionism? Was that normal? There was my anger when Simone or the children put a book in the wrong place on the shelf, when a light in a vacant room was left on. Short-lived but terrible anger. Simone, always wanting to hold the family together, must have rationalized all this away over the years, telling herself even a perfectionist isn't perfect. Most of the time I think I was fun to be around, and she could live with that.

I admired Simone's devotion to family and her survivor spirit. She and her family had been through a great deal during the Civil Rights years. Simone had single-handedly integrated Ludvigson High School in Louisiana. When she spoke about the experience, her eyes sparkled with the glow of acute recollection. Police officers had to escort her into the classroom on that first class day and sit around her in a circle just in case somebody acted stupid. That night, members of the KKK parked their vehicles in front their house and began to advance along the driveway. Mr. Williams anchored his shotgun on a window sill and the bullets sent the encroaching killers scurrying back to the road. By the time of her graduation, nearly a quarter of the children attending Ludvigson were Black. Simone had, no doubt, been schooled in the art of overcoming.

My moods and detachments one day prompted Simone to ask if I was seeing another woman. She'd asked directly, in her matter-of-fact manner, and that one time had been enough. Enough for a woman who knows when her man is cheating. Simone told me that she belonged to that class of women who knows. Even if she finds no hidden condoms, no implicating messages scribbled on receipts, no brushes of lipstick on his jackets or shirts, no strands of hair on his jackets, she knows if he's cheating. Taking a shower before returning home may remove the strange woman's odour, but will condemn him still. A woman knows the scent of a shower not taken at home. She knows the smell of all things. I knew what Simone was saying, but straying had not been one of my crimes.

'It's the little things that I'll miss,' I once overheard her telling a friend on the telephone. 'Like the way he likes his food very spicy, and how I'd cook it that way, placing tooth picks in the spicier portions of meat to mark them from the rest.'

'Huh-huh,' I imagined the friend saying.

'We had good times. He could be so much fun. The way he played around with words. I remember one afternoon at the mall, he said, "Let's take the lift." And I said, "You mean the elevator." Another time, when we got back from the supermarket, he asked me if I'd taken out everything from the car's boot. I said, "You mean the car trunk? Bootie means something else over here, Honey." And I put my hands on my buttocks and shook them. The two of us just fell about laughing. Oh, we had some very good times, Carissa.'

All that laughter had been drained from her. She was a stream that bubbled no more. All that remained was the weight of my accusations. I'd accused her of contradicting me, of trying to control me. I'd constantly perceived her responses as a correction, as a reprimand, as an insistence on being right all the time. I realize now I was wrong. My social difficulties in fitting in with many Americans, Black and White alike, had me on edge, had me constantly on guard. And there was no Caribbean community to speak of in Augusta, no real cultural support system. Simone had been rare, special. I'm sure her openness and ability to engage deeply with other races and classes, was honed by her exposure to other cultures during the programs of Study Abroad she'd attended as an undergraduate. She'd visited India, Africa, England, and Brazil, and these experiences, coupled with her own background (her paternal grandfather was a Cajun Frenchman, her mother part Cherokee) made her open to the world. This multicultural outlook was certainly one of the things that attracted me. But I was determined not to let anyone put me to sit in a corner, not to be second-class to anyone. And this was part of the social war I felt I was engaged in in my daily interactions with Americans.

I'd grown to see that the common skin colour of Blacks here and in the Caribbean is a deception, that it creates the mistaken assumption of shared identity, whereas the differences are in fact significant: in socialization, sense of humour, perceptions and ways of relating to Whites, and so on. Even though a good many African and Caribbean people are members of Black American churches, few of these make any effort to play music from Africa or the Caribbean, nor invite African or Caribbean ministers to preach. No one ever thinks to add jerk chicken or cou-cou to their banquet menus. Outside of the church world, the pattern is much the same. No Caribbean or African food or music at office parties. I'd discussed these issues with Simone earlier in our courtship and marriage, and she'd been most supportive. She, indeed, cautioned me that Americans were not as open as Third World folks, were more casual about relationships, that my expectations were too high for this country. But perhaps all this time away from my sandy shores had weakened me. Perhaps the issues I had to deal with daily in America had taken their toll. Perhaps, as a result, I'd become extreme, even irrational in my social anxieties. I had to protect my psyche, my ego. I had to.

So Simone had made her decision, had come to realize that all she understood of me was what was tangible, visible. There was a dimension to my life which she had never seen, smelt, touched. For her my past was a fleshless corpse. There were only the bones of my life, a stack of historical facts that could be found in a registry. She did not know the full spirit of my past, although at first I had wanted her to know – but this openness did not last long. For our honeymoon, she'd suggested Barbados. We got married in December, the height of the tourist season there. I told her all the flights had been taken right through until mid-January. So we honeymooned in Miami instead. For several years after we had been married, I had expressed my desire to go home. Simone had enthusiastically supported this idea. But, at the last minute, I'd always find an excuse not to go, usually a work-related one, and particularly the pressures of being just about to, or just having moved. The last time Simone pressed me had been about a year ago when Aunt Lolita left Barbados to live in New York. I told her I'd been away from the island for over fifteen years and would first have to go there on my own in order to check things out. That was how that conversation ended.

Her mother had been sceptical about me from the start. Much as I had hated to admit it, Mrs. Williams, and now Simone, was right on the subject of my past. Simone had no emotional sense of my life on the island. Even though she had suggested an unresolved issue in the past as one possible reason for my behaviour, the suggestion had been speculative, theoretical. All she had, all I'd given her, was a mist, a grey coiling mist, at best an intellectual outline: my love of music, emigration to America, my parents' deaths in a car accident during my last undergraduate year, my excuses for not returning home since coming to America. I remember after my parents died how Simone begged me to go home for the funeral, even offering to loan me the airfare. And not only Simone, but Aunt Lolita as well had predicted I'd regret not going. They were both right. Lord knows, I have suffered many sorrows as a result of not returning, not saying goodbye to all my blood. It struck me now that Simone might have pitied me. Had she mistaken pity for true love and formed a bond that should never have been? Had my pride and career been to her pitiful masks over a crying, vulnerable spirit? What was true was that my weakness had sucked her down into itself, had plunged her and the children into a life of instability. It had become increasingly difficult for me to bear the pain I was causing them. Something had to give. Deciding not to move with me had become Simone's only sane choice. It had come to that.

These were painful thoughts. My book and its contents called.

CHAPTER SIX

Just then, the doorbell rang. Simone shouted, 'Martin's here, Alphonso!' Unwillingly, I returned my aunt's letter to its paper tomb. Reluctantly, I descended the staircase.

'I got an hour to kill, guys,' I heard Martin Donovan say.

'Well, why don't you come up here and help me get down this desk and filing cabinet, Old Man,' I said, coming to a halt in the middle of the staircase.

'Old Man?' Martin had turned his head towards my voice. He rushed to the stairs with his fists raised, feigning anger. I continued my descent.

'And who's upstairs reading books while his wife's downstairs doing all the man's work?' Martin was now right in front of me and I realized I still held the book in my hand and a panic, that I tried hard to disguise, sent me scurrying back upstairs. Martin felt I had entered his game.

'It's no use hiding it now. I've already seen it,' he said laughing.

I had reeled into the present with my past. I had to get my past back into its place, where only I had access to it. Moving quickly to the bookcase, I placed the book on the shelf from where I had taken it, wiped my perspiring palms on my jeans and breathed deeply in an attempt to restore my calm before Martin joined me in the den.

Now he put his left arm around my shoulder, slapped me briskly and then we vigorously shook hands.

'What's happening, Martin? Good to see you too.' Martin was a real estate agent, a six-foot redhead with the rugged demeanour of the models in the Marlboro cowboy ads. Shaved, lined, rustic face. We had met at the Family Fitness Center nearly a year ago, some months after I had moved to Martinez. He had spent the last year trying to persuade me to buy a home instead of renting one. This was a provoking challenge to my tenacious friend.

'Look at this,' he pursued. 'Do you know what a profit you could've made on this baby, *if* it were yours?' He paced the den, gesturing toward the walls.

'Doesn't matter now, does it,' I said. Then I began singing an impromptu calypso.

I'm leaving this place come Monday,
I'm leaving, no matter what you say.
Over to Savannah, Martin'll follow me
With his old worn-out song:
'Buy Your Own Property.'
Oiiiieeeeee!!

I waved my hands in the air and gyrated my hips to an imaginary calypso rhythm. Martin tried to be serious and said, 'Funny. Real funny.'

I said, 'You like it? I know you do. Here's another one for you...'

You real estate fellas are all millionaires,
You make twice as much as we engineers.
So, don't mock me, don't lock me, 'cause if I buy a home,
It'll be one made of island limestone.
Oiiiieeeeeee!!

'How you like me, Martin?' I said. 'How you like me?'
'Pleeeeeeeease, Alphonso. This *can't* be the way Barbadi-

83

ans behave. You're a disgrace to your country. Darn, Alphonso,' he said, trying hard not to give in to laughter, 'you're wasting your life renting instead of owning. Think of the write-offs, will yuh? Granted, it's not the best time for selling, but it's a helluva good time for buying right now. The buying market's on the upswing, my man.' By now, Martin had conquered his urge to laugh. His intense brown eyes shone with the confidence of a salesman.

'I'm just not ready yet, Martin,' I sing-sang. 'When I am, you'll be the first to know. Trust me.'

'Boy, have I heard that one before.' he said.

I had told Martin of Simone's decision to stay in Martinez, and he'd told me I was losing a good woman. There was no way he could understand why I had to keep moving, and we had never become so close that I felt able to confide in him.

I had met Martin the first evening I worked out at Family Fitness. I had completed three sets (each of twenty-five reps) of bench presses, flyes, lateral pull-downs, long pulley rows, leg curls, leg extensions, and French curls. When I went over to the bicep machine, it was occupied by a tall sweating red-headed man wearing brown boxer shorts. I stood next to the machine awaiting my turn. After completing one of his sets, the man gestured for me to use the machine. We continued in this way, exchanging the equipment with alternate sets, until we had each completed all of our sets. In between the iron pumping we must have said a few things to each other, and, when we were through, Martin Donovan formally introduced himself and asked, 'Where're you from, man? Ethiopia?'

I laughed and said, 'You know, since I've been in the States, several people have asked me that same question. My pre-slavery ancestors must be from there. I'm from Barbados. Now, that's way down South, the nearest of the Windward Islands to Africa too – as the slaves fly.'

Martin laughed loudly, seemingly impressed by my

curious wit. He slid off his weight gloves and bent down to put them in his duffle bag.

'I love your music, mon,' he said in a bubble gum voice and looked up at me. 'Especially reggae. Don't have any of my own, but I love it when I hear it. It has the oomphf.'

'The what?' I asked. I had never heard the expression before.

'The oooommmmmmmmmphf,' Martin said with greater relish. 'It's hot, mon. Hot.'

Although Martin had said the word 'mon' before, I suddenly flushed at the way he said it. It was as if he was trying a little too hard to identify with me, or even (consciously or unconsciously) ridiculing my culture. I put my own gloves in my duffle and felt a growing prompting to zip my rummaging thoughts. Unsure of the dual echoes in Martin's tone, I drew the zipper and said, 'Hey, Martin. Remember one thing... I'm not your mum.' We headed out of the fitness centre with Martin's loud laughter ringing across the parking lot.

'I'll remember that,' he said. His laughter erased the implications of his tone and allayed my fears. I started laughing as well and we shook hands. Laughter of self-recognition that would form the basis of our friendship: mutual verbal mischief, like brothers close in age playfully giving each other a hard time.

It wasn't long before we were shooting pool together once a week. One Friday evening, we'd arranged to meet at Martin's house three miles away on Myrtle Drive. He'd earlier suggested we go to a nearby pool hall and bar and then, later, take in some live music. When I arrived at his tree-lined, two-storey, redbrick house, the six o'clock May sunlight waltzed softly over beds of yellow daffodils and pink azaleas. Dogwoods frothed around the house.

The Victorian style of the house reminded me somewhat of the Simpsons' house which I had visited once or twice with my father. But instead of red bricks, theirs were made of limestone, and instead of dogwoods, azaleas and daffodils, the Simpsons' house was shrouded with mahogany trees, flamboyants, royal palms, and allamandas. On one of these visits, I remember helping my father load a floral couch in his car that the Simpsons no longer needed. I recall saying hello to two or three of the Simpson sons who were wandering about the courtyard as we came out with the couch. I remember how awkward I felt at the gulf between us. A brief greeting was all that was possible. We had no common ground for further conversation. On another occasion, I remembered helping my father load a few boxes of books. A tall dark-skinned woman in a white apron and head dress was sweeping the yard. I remember how striking a contrast it was between her deep ebony skin and the white apron and head dress. What I could not forget from those visits was the shame and humiliation I felt at taking the Simpsons' used items. The feeling of having hot and cold water simultaneously running beneath my skin would assail me, especially as I loaded the items into the car. I felt an enormous relief as we drove out of the cobbled yard.

I pulled into the wide driveway and parked next to a red Corvette. I got out and looked up at the canopy of pines, oaks, and ash that sheltered the dogwoods. The blue eyes of the sky peered through the taller trees, some of which must have been at least sixty years old. The large, double-pillared house looked like old Georgia money. I kept expecting to see a gardener or a maid. But I wasn't intimidated. It was the kind of house I secretly dreamed of owning. Historical justice or levelling: I was all for it! There had been many houses this size in Barbados but made of coral stone instead of red bricks. Even before I emigrated to America, some affluent Blacks were living in such homes purchased from the children of the planter class. The Barbados Prime Minister lived in a house twice as big as this on at least three acres of land.

A woman, presumably Martin's wife, answered the door-bell. Brunette, blue-eyed and conservatively dressed, she held open the door in a tight-lipped manner. Martin had spoken of her, but this was my first time meeting her. She was clearly expecting me.

'You must be Alphonso,' she said. I nodded. She introduced herself as Jennifer, Martin's wife. 'Well, come on in. Martin'll soon be down. Have a seat. Can I get you something to drink?'

'No, thanks. I'm fine,' I said, sitting down on a blue floral couch. Her stiff cordiality made me uncomfortable. I looked up into the ceiling to find an escape. A magnificent chandelier, like crystal teardrops, hung there. I looked down again to see a little red-headed girl, about Lucinda's age, pass in front of me. Like Hamlet to Ophelia, she kept her eyes glued on me until she passed out of the room. Martin appeared with a loud, 'How're you doin'?' I got up to greet him. The little redhead passed by again.

'You're black,' she said. She stopped right in front of me and folded her arms.

'Elizabeth,' Martin scolded mildly, 'this is my friend, Alphonso. He's not from here. He's from Barbados. We'll look it up on the map a little later, OK?'

'OK,' the girl said, accepting her father's recommendation with a giggle.

'Elizabeth,' I said, wearily putting on my social mask. 'That's such a pretty name.' But even as I said this, I felt the old mixture of hot and cold water run underneath my skin. I had heard it said that some Americans treated foreign Blacks with greater respect than American Blacks. The girl's acceptance of me following Martin's geographical reassurance, seemed to confirm this view. Was I being oversensitive? Was I overreacting to what was an honest inquiry from a child who, for the first time perhaps, had seen a Black person in her home? Was the child's comment an innocent attempt at conversation with a stranger? Was Martin's statement simply information given to educate his daughter?

These encounters were, in one form or another, much more frequent here than in Barbados where the White population was so much smaller, some three percent. No-one could escape the face of race in America. It was evident wherever you turned, at school, at work, in the media. When different races met, the first thought was always of that difference, the first sensation always a consciousness of colour. I couldn't escape this reality however much I abhorred it.

No tall, dark-skinned uniformed maid showed. Martin and I left in his Corvette and headed for the pool hall and bar over in the Plaza. There the bartender smiled broadly at us and said, 'How're y'all doin' today?' Martin raised a hand in response. I indicated I was doing fine with a firm nod and simultaneous opening and closing of my mouth.

It was a typical bar: subdued lighting, a monitor on the wall (now emitting a news update) installed primarily for the viewing of ball games; a constant subterranean hum of conversation punctuated by the occasional howl, the raucous laugh. We ordered two draft beers. Martin insisted on paying for them. Then we headed down a hallway to the pool room at the rear of the building. Several pinball machines stood like sentries at the sides of the room, and I heard the launch of inter-galactic wars. One man with large tattooed arms clutched the handle bars and grimaced with intensity. Every now and again he hollered, 'Gotcha!' and slapped his right hand against the machine's thigh. The pool room was much less crowded than the bar area – about fifteen people in all. When the tattooed warrior looked at me, all the other alien eyes in the room immediately seemed to follow suit. For a moment, all went silent. My thoughts scurried like the striped balls on the lawn-green tables. As Martin and I approached the table, the balls in my head scurried faster when an overweight middle-aged man, wearing blue jeans and a sweater, and carrying a pool cue, swished toward us.

'Hey, Martin. What's goin' on?' the hefty man said. 'Still selling all those houses?' He was right next to us. His fat flesh seemed to settle on him when he came to a stop. The collective eye divided into pairs and refocused on their respective table tops. The clanking of the balls resumed.

'You're kidding, Greg,' Martin said. 'Don't you see all those *For Sale* signs up everywhere in Augusta and over here? Nobody's buying. I wish you'd send some business my way.'

'Woah, woah. Just a minute now. That's not what I've been hearing.'

All this time, Greg looked through me as if I wasn't there. Martin seemed unaware of this. He addressed the other man as if everything was normal and in place.

'Well, actually, I'm survivin'. But just barely now.'

'Sure. Sure. I know you are. I guess every little bit really adds up, eh Martin? Well, take care y'self. Good seeing you.'

'You bet.'

The overweight body swished towards a table at the far corner of the room. I would not have come into a place like this alone. But I was with a white man whom I regarded as a friend, so let them stare, let them not see me. As long as none of them bothered me, I intended to enjoy my game and my beer. Maybe my friendship with Martin might contribute in some small way to more racial tolerance in these parts. Who knows? But I knew that this could only work both ways if Martin, in his turn, visited some of my haunts. Some time I intended to put all this to the test.

We spent an hour or so in the pool room and then went over to the Red Tiger in Augusta where we listened to a folk guitarist play and sing his heart out to an audience which grew progressively more drunk and inattentive as the night wore on. I remembered how it used to be. In a band, when the audience's attention slackened, you could play off of each other and still have a lot of fun. But to bare your soul to a crowd caught up in their own intoxication was the worst indignity a solo performer could suffer.

We left the Red Tiger around one o'clock, filled with beer and merriment. On the way to Martin's house, he said, 'You know, Alphonso, you're not like other Blacks around here, you know.' In spite of the alcohol, an uneasy feeling started creeping over me.

'You have a sense of humour,' he bubbled. 'You don't carry around a chip on your shoulder all the time. You got the oommmmmmmmphf, mon. And I like that.'

I was unsure how to respond, so I said nothing. What was it that troubled Martin? Or was it me who was overreacting? Why did I have this uncomfortable feeling Martin was trying too hard to identify with me? And why hadn't he introduced me to Greg? Was Martin an accomplice (whether consciously or unconsciously) in the old psychology of exclusion? I strained not to think of Martin in this manner. I liked Martin.

Next day, I raised some of these issues with Simone.

'Let me tell you somp'n,' she said, sitting cross-legged on the sofa and sipping a cup of herbal tea. 'Martin respects me 'cause I'm your wife, OK? But Martin's still typically White American (let me tell you what I mean).' She paused momentarily, and I couldn't help thinking that I knew her so well. I knew that I could count on her support in matters such as this, whenever any threat came from the outside into our lives. Her lips opened into a vowel of protection. 'OK. Some of them can't deal with Black Americans 'cause we remind them too directly of their ancestors' crimes, OK? The ones who still have some sensitivity, hook up with someone like yourself (a West Indian or an African, right?), so they can tell themselves: "I have a Black friend, so I'm no bigot." But, in the end, it all smacks of patronage. There's still some line drawn as to how far they'll embrace you...'

'He's always telling me I'm not like other Blacks here,' I said. I sensed that some revelation was in the air. Simone's braided hair seemed to bristle with it. My right foot involuntarily began rubbing the instep of the left foot like stray cat scratching on a door. I starved for some clear answers. Even though I'd been in America all this time, I could never quite come to terms with the nature of race relationships. In Barbados, race invariably went along with class differences. The Simpsons and my family were divided by power. Here Martin and I were both professionals. I probably earned much more than Greg in that bar. Here it was race pure and simple, but all the more perplexing for that. When it was overt and obvious, I understood it clearly and intellectually. But when it came with subtlety and nuance I had no tools other than my emotions. It gave me a headache to try to figure it out. It simply wasn't my style to think in such terms.

'That's exactly what I'm saying,' Simone said. 'What he means is that you're no threat to his deep-seated prejudices, because you're from another country and not right in his yard. He don't have to go through the discomfort of real change. He don't have to deal with that, while at the same time he has you as a buffer for his conscience. You see what I'm saying?'

I didn't like where the conversation was heading nor my growing discomfort, but I was determined to see it through. The telephone rang. I walked over and answered it. 'Who?' I asked and hung up. Then I walked over and sat on the black leather recliner and said to Simone, 'Alfred, the phone is for you.'

'Silly,' she said and smiled. But she quickly aborted the levity. She seemed anxious to get some beast off her chest. 'But as I was saying... I'd be careful if I were you. It's not that

I don't like Martin. I do. He's funny. The kids like him. And you obviously fill a need in his life and vice-versa. But it's not Martin all by himself. He's a family man, so that includes his wife, his family, and other friends. You see what I mean?'

'Yes, I see.'

'Fancy his child looking at you and calling you black. Of course, you're black. But already the racial consciousness is in that child. All I'm saying, Alphonso, is don't put your expectations too high, 'cause I know how seriously you take friendships. I don't want you get yourself hurt.'

I got up with a sigh and said, 'I hear you.'

I went into the kitchen, opened the fridge door and took out a Heineken, uncapped it, and drank a third of it in one gulp. This calmed me some. When I returned to the living room, Simone was sipping the last of her tea.

'It's funny,' I said, retaking my seat on the black recliner, 'but most Black guys I've met here, so far, seem just as provincial as the Whites. The only difference is one type of segregation's racial, the other's cultural. But, at least, people can choose now. I don't know. Maybe sticking to one's own is the best thing to do, after all. I don't know.'

'For us, the safest thing to do. It's called self-protection, Alphonso. Protection from abuse. Protection from the Beast.'

'I guess I can understand why Blacks here stick to themselves,' I said. 'Historical mistrusts have a way of forcing people into a reverse provincialism, I guess. But how do you explain segregation in a place like Barbados where the Blacks are in the majority?'

'You tell me.'

'Barbadian Whites hardly get involved in the social and cultural life of the place, but, unlike minorities here, they can afford to. Financially, I mean. Whites still control most of the wealth in Barbados, you know. Emotionally? Personally, I think white Barbadians are all quite mad. Money can't buy them peace. They live in fear, like hostages in their own country. What harms Blacks emotionally is the class segregation within the Black community.'

It suddenly struck me that I was speaking with confident authority as a Barbadian expatriate who hadn't been home in nearly sixteen years. But I felt I was on the right lines. Surely if there had been major changes in the social and economic structures of the island, Clarence would have told me. When Barbados became independent from Great Britain in 1966, Blacks had been content to have political power, Whites to retain financial power. Racial coexistence had been established along these lines. I could not recall a single major racial incident in Barbados during my nineteen years there. The Black middle class, many of whom worked for White-owned companies, had been the most visible source of irritation for the majority of other Black Barbadians.

Simone said, 'You get that here too, but certainly snobbery's not as valid a reason to perpetuate separatism as racism is.'

'I don't think any kind of segregation's good, mind you. And I don't think Black Americans should separate themselves from other ethnic groups because of their bad experiences with Whites. But you're absolutely right,' I said, warding off what I sensed was a gathering odour of argument. 'And the results are the same. Always the same. Every crab in his own hole.'

Simone smiled her protective smile and slowly shook her head from side to side.

'I like that,' she said. 'And it's so true. Every crab in his own hole.'

Martin and I maintained our boys' night out and, after a few weeks, I decided it was time to put my plan to the test. I invited him to go with me to Super B Night Club in Augusta. As much as Simone had penetrated my consciousness with her theories on race, I was still unprepared for Martin's response. I extended the invitation one Wednesday evening as we were leaving the fitness centre.

'No way!' was Martin's instantaneous response. He appeared horrified. 'That's over in South Augusta. You don't want to go into that part of town. You won't want to go in there with those expensive suede shoes. Someone could kill you for them.'

He said all this in almost one breath. His horror was real, earnest, perhaps even well-meaning. A friend's warning? Simone's words banged in my brain. This was how White Americans saw the world: Black and White, them and us. Caribbean Black was more acceptable than American Black. It all seemed so ridiculous. I couldn't take it any more. Battle lines were drawn. It was war. I stopped walking and said, 'Look, Martin. I go to your pool halls, your clubs, your bars. I've seen tattooed men and women in them who looked like hardened criminals, so don't give me this bull-shit 'bout "that part of town." If I can hang in your joints, you should be able to hang in mine, otherwise this friendship ain't worth a damn. I mean, if you feel that way 'bout Black people, why bother with me, man?'

'I already told you you're different...'

'I'm sick of hearing that crap, man. My experience may be different, but the history's the same: slavery, the whole lot. I don't have a chip on my shoulder (as you say) only because where I'm from ninety-five percent of the people are of my race and Blacks have been ruling since the sixties. I see people as people. But, maybe, if I'd grown up in this country, I'd probably be just like "those other people" you talk so much about!'

'OK, OK, OK,' Martin said, his voice lowering to almost a whisper. 'You've made your point.'

We stood in the middle of the parking lot, just a few yards from our cars which were parked not far from each other.

A few passers-by observed our altercation with momentary curiosity. Others increased their walking pace. Dusk had gathered around the buildings of the plaza, and the head-lights of cars on the neighbouring highway were speeding fireflies. We stood there flushed, silent, and tense. Then, without any further words, we strode toward our respective cars, not once looking back.

Two weeks later, Martin called.

'I have a confession to make,' he began. I said nothing, still in a state of mistrust. I waited for him to speak again. He told me about his extreme conservative upbringing; how, in high school he, too, was guilty of racial intolerance, participating in racial jokes and such like. He had married his conservative childhood sweetheart. And then the shocking disclosure: his grandfather's associations with the Klan. His grandfa-ther, a councilman, had risen to the position of Cyclops, which meant he was a leader of the local KKK organization. When he was sixteen, Martin remembered attending a huge Klan rally in Plains, Georgia. He described the scene as if it were happening at that moment. He described the large field behind a farm where the hooded members and the non-hooded guests had gathered. The cars had come slith-ering down the dirt road next to the farm and were parked, in hedgerow fashion, around the field. Huge oaks, curtained with Spanish moss, bordered the field like guards. Martin described walking through patches of grapevine and pal-metto in order to get to the clearing where a platform had been erected. In front of the platform, mainly old men, women, and children sat in plastic chairs arranged in a semicircle. Everyone else stood up. His grandfather had made him sit in a front row seat, and he remembered having to endure a pelvic itch for the length of the meeting. Much to his relief, the meeting was aborted when, halfway through, a man, hoping to disrupt the proceedings, rammed a Jaguar sports car into the speakers' platform injuring a few bystanders and sparking a melee. Later, at home, he discovered a tick in his underwear.

'I'll never forget what a local farmer said to me on the way out from the meeting,' Martin said. 'He asked me: "Why have you brought all this trouble to Plains?" That made me think real hard. Real hard. I never went to another meeting and vowed, there and then, that I'd try to be different. It wasn't easy. When I was in college, I joined the Reserves and worked under Black men.'

I began to feel somewhat disarmed by Martin's confessions, as if I was being drawn into some strange purgatorial web. All these experiences, he said, had made him more tolerant of Blacks, but he was not perfect. No person was. He was still a product of a particular upbringing and culture. It seemed to me as if he had his own historical burden, and I now understood what Simone had meant about me filling a need in his life. It was hard work shedding the skin of one's old nature. People needed help in that regard. Maybe I was unconsciously helping Martin deal with his past. But who would help me deal with mine?

Martin had broken down and was big enough to share his ghost with me. Ghost grandfather for Martin. Ghost brother for me. These were, no doubt, personal unities beyond and within the racial graveyard. But they could not be shared. I would not break down. I would never tell him about my ghost, my Elroy.

'We're going out on Friday night,' Martin said.

'Where?'

'Super B.'

'You're on, man,' I said. 'But leave the ticks at home.'

CHAPTER SEVEN

Martin left. I know he felt uncomfortable in our house now, about intruding into a private grief. He couldn't make sense of what I was doing, how I could separate from Simone and risk losing the girls in this way. Despite all that had passed between us, I still could not open up to him. There was a forced jollity in our repartee that couldn't cover the fact that our relationship had also come to an end.

I ascended the staircase and took up the novel again. I opened it as though I were turning open a gate in myself. Gate of a letter creaking open in Aunt Lolita's handwriting, postmarked, Bridgetown, Barbados, May 7, 1984. One week before my twenty-third birthday. It was my final semester in LSU's Bachelor of Science program. Aunt Lolita wrote:

> Dear Alphonso:
>
> I hope this letter finds you in good health and will give you fuller details on your nice mum's and nice dad's deaths which my call last week couldn't give. I'm so sorry you couldn't come home for the funeral. Naturally, everyone asked for you, and I had to explain you were on scholarship and not far from graduation, so you couldn't attend. Of course, I must tell you I still feel you should've tried harder to make some

sort of arrangement so you could attend your parents' funeral. Any university would have understood how important it was for you to come home at that time. And what if you had to repeat a semester? Four months! What is four months compared to eternity? But you're a man now, and you made your decision. I just hope you can live with it.

Anyway, as I was saying, Aunt E and Fitz had a lovely turnout. Tons of people. You would have thought it was a politician's funeral or some big-shot lawyer or something. St. Paul's was packed like sardines. Only one long-distance relative, one Verona (who is really only a Hutson by name), acted like a real jackass, hollering out to the top of her voice, 'Fitzgerald! Fitzgerald! O Lord, not Fitzgerald!' when they started to bring the caskets out of the church. She made such a scene, hear? Holding her belly and hollering like if she did really hurt. Some people just have to get noticed.

Anyway, I got a white coffin for your nice dad. That's what I know he would have wanted. The only real breaks he ever got were from white people. Even before he started driving for the Simpsons, through Aunt E, he got a loan to buy the land the house was on. Just six months before that, old Mr. Simpson bought a new car and let Fitzy keep the five-year-old Corolla wagon as a gift. Those were proper people. Proper people. It's such a pity Fitzy had to leave us so soon. Some people never get to live to enjoy the things God put on this earth for us. You know, he was driving to the airport when the madness happen. Aunt E never flew on a plane in her life and Fitz had convinced her to go for a holiday with him up to New York to stay with my mother, your Aunt Evangie. He was treating his wife when the madness happen. Life's so funny, so unfair, but God knows best.

My mother helped raised him, you know. Before she emigrated to the States. His father was a no-good red-nigger man and his mother, my sister Ilene, died when Fitz was three. Ilene was the prettiest out of my mother's three girl children. Like me, she could have almost pass for white. But she mixed herself up with the wrong men, men who couldn't do nothing for her. So she spent her short life behind a sewing machine, stitching away her life. You know, my first husband's brother wanted to marry her, you know. If my first husband had two plantations, then his brother, Patrick, had four. Proper people. Proper people. But your father's father like he turned Ilene foolish or something. All she wanted was Archibald, a no-good good-for-nothing rum drinker. She could have been somebody today. And with her beauty... She had hair, long and jet-black, reaching down to her waist. Straight nose. Proud full lips. Skin smooth like silk and fairer than mine.

Anyway, Alphonso, I buried you nice mum in a brown coffin. They both looked so peaceful, so lovely in their coffins, Alphonso. I took care of everything. You know how I am about family. Your father was the only real blood-relative I had left on the island. You know, Ronald became a Christian, closed his practice here, and is now in Bible College in Philadelphia, and all my other close relatives are in New York. So, I don't know. I promised your father I'd look out for Elroy if anything ever happened, and I will honour that. The doctor don't give him much time anyway. A few months ago, he developed some kind of sarcoma cancer. And no wonder. With all that medicine they've pumped into him over the years. I'll try and get a tenant for your house. While I'm here, I'll look after that, but if and when I leave here, Alphonso, you'll have to take responsibility for the property, hear? Your father really maintained the house very well. It's a beautiful little house, and it now belongs to you. You understand?

Bronze also gone. Three days after the accident, I found him curl up in the yard by the shed. Poor old Bronze.

I hope you're not taking on what happened too hard.

Remember, we Hutsons are fighters, you know. So, don't give up. Try to have a happy birthday, and good luck with your exams.

With love,
Your Aunt Lolita

When Aunt Lolita's phone call had come the week before, I'd been studying in my redbrick apartment on Azalea Street. It was about five o'clock in the evening, bright light, a blue sky, the temperature in the eighties. I had shut off the air conditioner and had opened the back door to let the steady breeze sweep through the house. Seated at the book-covered dining table, I saw the bright afternoon light hug the houses across the street where my college mate, Angus, had an apartment.

I picked up the phone, and immediately sensed a hesitancy in Aunt Lolita's voice. She was not given to hesitancy, and that was why it had been so noticeable. Her voice carried the cautionary tone of a bearer of bad news. How was I? Was I all right? *Sit down. I have something to tell you.* I thought something was wrong, especially since she kept repeatedly asking me if I was all right. Even before she told me there had been an accident, a lump had started to form in my throat. By the time she had finished conveying the news, I had broken down in huge heaving sobs. I heard myself reply that I couldn't get away for the funeral, because I was nearing the end of my final semester. I caught Aunt Lolita's reprimand.

'What will people think, Alphonso? It's your parents. You only have one set of parents in the world, and this'll be the last chance you'll get to see them. If you don't come, you'll regret this later on.'

I tried to explain my financial situation. The scholarship funds were just enough to cover tuition, the monthly $350.00 rent on the one-bedroom apartment, food, utilities, and heath insurance.

'The University will understand,' Aunt Lolita said. 'I'm sure they'll let you do whatever make-ups you need when you get back.' I told her I wanted to come but that I simply couldn't afford to do so. When she didn't offer to pay my airfare or loan me the money, I said goodbye and hung up the phone.

I recalled my father saying how Aunt Lolita never gave or loaned money to anyone. She'd give you ground provisions and fruits from her late husbands' plantations. After their deaths, she'd kept the estates running by hiring managers and by diversifying the crops to include fruits and vegetables. She'd give away her used clothes to less fortunate family members, including my mother who was close to her in size. But everyone, said my father, knew not to ask her for money.

I loved my parents when they were alive, and they knew that. I felt that, under the circumstances, there was no need to miss my finals and set back my academic career just to conform to social expectations or just to please tightfisted Aunt Lolita.

Still dazed and confused, I dialled Simone's number. We had been dating for nine months now, although it seemed like years. She made the twenty-minute drive from off Airline Highway in about twelve minutes. I opened the door. When she came in, I found it impossible to look her straight in the face. This was the first time I had ever been so shattered, so vulnerable in her presence. The strange sense of nakedness which I felt caused me to veer away when she approached me with her outstretched arms. One hand managed to touch my shoulder, and that touch, as soft as it was, cut the cord of my emotions like a knife blade.

I remembered shouting to Simone, 'Tell me it's not true! Tell me it's not true!' and falling into her arms. My body weakened, and I slid to the floor. I couldn't believe they were both dead. They couldn't be. Aunt Lolita must have been mistaken. How could they have done this to me? How could they both have left me at the same time? It just wasn't fair. It was not supposed to be like that. I was yelling at Simone, at the walls, at the phone. Then I broke down in uncontrollable tears. I clutched at my stomach as if to stop the tears, but they just flowed out endlessly.

Simone remained standing, silent. When I calmed some, she stooped down beside me and placed her hand on my chest, telling me everything would be all right and softly, in even metre, patting my chest.

'Stay with me tonight,' I said, sitting up and sniffing heavily. Simone helped me to my feet and led me to the bedroom. I was as bent as a decrepit old man. She drew back the covers and helped me out of my clothes and into my pyjamas.

'I'll make you some hot tea, Honey. You take it easy. You lie down and rest yourself.' I did as I was told and crept under the covers. Simone turned to go into the kitchen. I watched her quietly leave the room and soon heard the tinkling of wares coming from the kitchen.

I tried to divert myself from the tragic news by scouring the room for comforts. Next to me, in a photograph on the side table, Simone made faces as she prepared to bite into a chicken leg. Our first Christmas together, last year at her apartment. I gazed over to the left where my Yamaha guitar leaned on its stand. On that wall hung one of Simone's paintings, a watercolour of White and Black students screaming and gesturing at each other in LSU's Quadrangle. The figures, though excessively exaggerated and distorted to create a comic effect, made a telling political point.

None of these things comforted me. I was conscious of a strange smell in the room. It could have been my own perspiration or breath. It could have been the tea brewing in the back. All I kept thinking was that it smelt like death.

Next morning, after a restless night, I thought about

asking Simone to loan me the money to buy the airline ticket home. But even when she beat me to it by offering to lend me the money, my intentions recoiled and wouldn't allow me to accept the offer. I wouldn't go to the funeral. I was too close to graduation, too close to the partial fulfilment of my goal. Goal of security. I *had* to succeed in America. All that Barbados was able to offer me were ghosts of one kind or another. I had loved my parents when they were alive, and they knew that. My presence at the funeral wouldn't add or subtract anything. If this had happened during one of the breaks, I would have gone home even if it meant putting myself in debt. But not now. Not on the threshold of my graduation. What difference would it make whether or not I went to the funeral? Wasn't I paying my respects in the way I felt and the grief I bore? So I resisted Simone's attempts to persuade me to change my mind.

Months turned to years after my parents' deaths. I gained my masters in 1986 and went to work for Wesslar two months after graduation. At that time, it seemed that almost every conversation, silently with myself or with Simone, contained direct or implied references to my parents: the values they represented of charity, discipline, courage, and hard work, values I wanted to pass on to our children. And whenever I spoke of my parents, tears gathered in my eyes. Occasionally, I'd weep aloud.

That year I still couldn't believe they were gone. I had spoken to my mother just a week before the accident, and I remembered how lively she sounded. Perhaps if I'd been there, living on the island near them, I could have saved them. Simone told me to stop blaming myself, that there was nothing I could do, whether or not I was in the island, and that it was not my fault. I began to feel as if, somehow, I was in some way wronged. It seemed so unfair that they had to die when I wasn't there to hold their hands, to say goodbye. I stared helplessly at Simone. She said, 'Leave it alone, Alphonso. There was nothing you could do. Their time had come to go on, that's all. Just leave it alone.'

A year after my parents' burial, in a letter postmarked Bridgetown, Barbados, August 24, 1985, Aunt Lolita wrote:

My Dear Alphonso:

I'm sorry to be the bearer of bad news again. Our family goes from one set of bad news to another. Something must have happened back in the family a long time ago, something bad, some curse. It shouldn't come as too much of a shock to you to know that Elroy's dead. He passed away quietly on the 23rd which would be about ten days before you got this letter. I didn't bother to call because, as you know, the long-distance phoning costs a lot of money and, knowing the situation with Elroy, I didn't think it necessary to call. Naturally, there were no public obituary announcements. He was buried at Westbury. He couldn't be buried with your nice mum and nice dad, because their graves were still too fresh, so they had to put him in the nearest available spot in the unmarked section. Because there was no way to purchase a spot for him, it means that we can't cast any concrete around the grave (in a few years, they'll have to re-use the spot, you see?). But I got permission from the cemetery people to put a wooden cross with an inscription so that when you *finally* get to Barbados, you'll know where he is buried. The cemetery people did a professional job. I buried him early in the morning. The only people around were the weeders. So, I've kept my promise to your father.

I may not be in the island for very much longer now. As soon as I'm able to sell my home, I plan to join my mother, your great aunt Evangie, in New York. All my close family in the States now. And you, poor boy. Alphonso, you really must get married. The young woman Simone you talked about sounds like a fine girl. With the depletion of the family, it rests with you to keep the Hutson name going, hear? (Laugh)

Of course, when I decide to leave, you'll have to come to Barbados and see after your house. How soon I'll be leaving, I don't know as yet. As I said, it all depends on the sale of my house. The tenants I got for you are a young married couple, and they seem to be good people – always pay on time. As long as I'm here in the island, I'll try to keep your house occupied so that the termites won't take over.

Write me soon, dear, and take care of yourself.

With love
Your Aunt Lolita

Aunt Lolita in fact stayed in Barbados for another ten years. She was determined to get BDS$220,000 for her BDS$175,000 house, and it was 1995, when property values increased, before she finally sold her house for BDS$200,000, and immediately made plans to leave the island. She implored me to come and see after my parents' house, because the current tenancy lease would expire a month after she left the island. She would be leaving in two months. She had made arrangements, through her lawyer, to have the last two months' rent deposited in the account that she had opened ten years ago in my name. The lawyer was also expected to ensure vacation of the premises after the current lease expired. She stressed how imperative it was for me to go to Barbados, meet the lawyer, and decide what I was going to do with the property. Sell it? Be an absentee landlord? She had kept her word to my father, and now it was time for me to shoulder my responsibilities like a man and take charge.

Unsure of my intentions about the property, I wrote and told Aunt Lolita not to renew the lease and to make sure that, before she left the island, she made arrangements to have the house boarded-up. Wrought iron doors should be installed over the existing ones for extra protection against vandals.

When she arrived in New York, she mailed me the house keys, and I kept them in a little leather pouch in the top right-hand corner of the mahogany chest. In the letter that came with the keys, she again urged me to go to Barbados and take care of business there. I even told Simone about Aunt Lolita's arrival in New York and of my decision to go to Barbados to see after the house. I even called to book the ticket, but called it off at the last minute. This fearful hesitancy invoked one of my failed boyhood rites of passage. To be regarded as a 'big-boy' and not a 'little-boy', I recalled, meant that I had to go to the end of the jetty on Brighton beach and jump into water at least forty feet deep. I would be determined to do it and then, at the last minute, hold back, seized by fright. I knew I had to jump into the water to lift my status among my friends. But the sight of the rolling waves and heaving water always paralysed me with fear. And this was the pattern for almost nine months after the tenants moved out. The lawyer had written to let me know that the house had been secured against vandals, though certainly not against termites. I thanked him in one of my briefest letters ever.

My last image of the house was in a photograph sent by my father in 1984, the same year he and my mother died. My father, in brown leather sandals, greyish pants, and pink long-sleeved shirt, had his right hand resting proprietorially on the blue bonnet of the second-hand Corolla station wagon. His back was erect, his left hand akimbo, and a broad toothy smile lit up his face. The house, a darker pink than his shirt, could be seen to the left, renovations completed. The house was small, exquisite in its simplicity. Part of the front hedge, burst with pink oleanders; Pride of Barbados, crotons, and red hibiscus, occupied the bottom right foreground. Two royal palms, wearing necklaces of red and green buds, erupted from the lawn, their fronds flowing like green fountains. My mother, no doubt, had been the photographer.

I thought of that photograph now, as I stared at the second letter, and I felt as if my heart would break. I had never said goodbye. There had been no ending. It was as if Elroy had never existed and always existed. I had no memories of playing with an elder brother on that neatly-trimmed lawn. Here was a house, a modest dwelling, but a symbol of all life's material achievement to the smiling man next to it. I realized that I did not share the peace in my father's face, even though I, too, had accomplished all the goals of surface accomplishment: a high-paying job, a wife, two lovely daughters. All this and yet I couldn't settle down. Every time I'd come close to doing so, the anemones stirred, a panic rose within me and the inevitable move splashed over onto my household. The children wanted to know what would become of their friends. Simone smouldered with frustration. Now, she was leaving me. That is what her decision to stay in Martinez meant. I would be alone, and I had only myself to blame.

I knew that I should go to the island. I sensed it was the only way to calm those restless anemones, my only chance, perhaps, to regain my family. I wanted to go. I was afraid to go. So much time had passed. There were active ghosts there waiting for me to put them to rest. I well knew the nature of my fears. To buy a house and settle down physically and emotionally, as other immigrants had done, would be like saying: my parents never existed. Elroy never existed. I had not seen their graves, had not said goodbye. I see impressions only, and I reel with pride or fear or guilt. I see a couple glorying in their sense of achievement. I see a wheelchair with a baby's fat cheeks. I need a name planted like a flag in the earth, a gravestone, a black wooden cross. I need to touch them with my own two hands.

PART TWO

CHAPTER EIGHT

Taking off from San Juan at five in the evening, the British West Indies Airways jet bored like a lonely silver fish through the cloudless afternoon sky. The sea's horizon and the sky line were indistinguishable, so that all the visible world had become one colour: blue. I had flown Delta from Augusta to Atlanta where I'd transferred to another Delta aircraft bound for San Juan. I had the good sense to travel light (two carry-ons; no check-through) having been forewarned by a Puerto Rican co-worker of the horrors of connections from Puerto Rico to other Caribbean destinations. Wendy Ortiz had painted a gloomy scenario of lost luggage, weeks of waiting for it, and impossible officials. Since my intention was to stay in Barbados for only three weeks, I decided not to tempt fate. If I needed more clothes I would buy them.

On the BWIA jet, I was reminded how long it was since I'd been to the Caribbean when I observed that almost half of the stewards were males. Friendly, well-worked-out bodies bulging from short-sleeved cotton shirts. No beards. Hair cut short.

The plane stopped in Antigua for about forty-five minutes to let off some tourists, and then flew over Barbados to Trinidad. There, a large group of Trinidadian youths boarded, carrying canvas sacks and book bags. The Indian, Black and *dougla* students laughed and talked in loud excited voices. I suspected they were heading back for a new term at Cave Hill. I felt a growing affinity with them. I, too, was heading back. But as the jet took off, I realized there was one great difference between us. They knew what they were going back to; I didn't. My elation fled.

Suddenly, in an attempt to extricate myself from the bad feelings that now possessed me, I reached up and pressed the service button. A half-Indian, half-Black stewardess arrived, smiling brightly. I ordered a rum and orange juice and she danced away down the aisle, my eyes following her slender body. After a few minutes, she returned with the order. She reached across the man and woman seated next to me, and I reached out and took the miniature bottle of Cockspur rum and the glass of orange juice with its napkin.

It was when the man next to me said, 'That's OK, man' after I'd apologised for the second time for reaching across him that it occurred to me that there was something curiously familiar about his features. Something stirred in my memory. Several times I tried to place him but finally gave up. I could tell from his voice he was a White Barbadian. The pitch of his voice was high, without tonal modulations but with a pronounced accent that unconsciously made statements sound like questions.

'Visiting home after nearly sixteen years,' I said to my neighbour. 'Must be a lot of changes, yes.'

'A fair amount. Tourism's still strong and we holding our own on the information highway. Barbados has the best telecommunications system in the whole Caribbean. And to top that, we won this year's Shell Shield Cricket Tournament. Not bad for a small island, eh.' The man spoke in a confident voice, laced with pride, the pride and confidence of someone with deep vested interests, an owner perhaps.

'Oh, by the way, I'm Alphonso Hutson,' I said, smiling and reaching for his hand.

'Good to meet you,' he returned. 'I'm Geoffrey...

112

Geoffrey Simpson and this is my wife Ann.' Ann, who had been reading a paperback, smiled in my direction.

'Simpson? Are you related to Simpson of Simpson Enterprises?'

'That's me,' he said, adjusting his gold-rimmed glasses.

'Your father was Maurice Simpson? Your mother Betty Simpson?'

'Yes.'

'You might not remember me, but I met you once – it must have been at least twenty years ago – at your father's house in Rockley. My parents both worked for your family.'

'You're Hutson's boy? My! What! Your mother had a hand in raising me, you know. Boy! What a coincidence! We all loved her, but she was strict when she had to be. And your father drove for us for years, until the accident.' Geoffrey Simpson suddenly stopped speaking, paddling through the straits of memory. I was re-paddling more vigorously than ever, especially now that I knew who he was. 'We missed Hutsy a lot. We were all very fond of him. So you were away all these years? What field are you in?'

'Engineering.'

'Hutsy would have been proud of you. You've done pretty well for yourself.'

'Fairly well,' I said. 'And how're your parents?'

'Well, my father passed away years now, but my mum's still alive,' Geoffrey said. I remembered my mother referring to Mrs. Simpson as a slave driver, but to Mr. Simpson as a man with a good heart. Had she been alive I could imagine her saying something such as 'De wicked like they does always outlive the good.'

Geoffrey Simpson and I continued talking, moving between personal memory and recent island history. I remembered the trips to his parents' house with my father to acquire the hand-me-down furniture and used books. And here I was, seated next to him, so close, so intimate, sharing the same air. In the past, all that was allowed was just a hello and a bye. It was tempting to think that time, education, and experience were levelling the old disparities of race and class, but I knew that this dialogue would probably be as far as our social interaction would go. During my years on the island, it was rare to find real mixing between Barbadian Blacks and Whites. There had never been any open racial hostility that I could remember, but the races largely kept to themselves. Interracial marriage was strenuously discouraged. It was as if there was an inveterate Victorian fear of scandal. Even if genuine feelings existed between the races, both Blacks and Whites were trained in the art of emotional suppression. The Black and White couples one saw on the island were invariably Black Barbadians and Whites from England, Europe, Canada, or America.

White students (and some Blacks from affluent families) who failed to gain entry to Lodge, Combermere, Harrison's College or Queen's College (the island's top public secondary schools) were sent to The Ursuline Convent, St. Gabriel's, St. Winifred's, Mapps or Presentation College where the fees for private tuition was high and distance from the mainly Black working-class children assured. Where there was a relationship between Whites and Blacks it was invariably that of employer and employee. However, the island had remained calm and the tourist and industrial development brochures touted it as politically stable and a prime location for foreign investors.

Around eight-thirty, I looked out the window and saw Barbados's southern shoulder swim into view. My heart jumped. I swallowed the rest of what was now my third drink and breathed deeply. I noticed that lights mottled this part of the island, flickering like candles in the dark. Uncertain wheels rose and fell inside me, sparking and hesitant to land.

But land we did. As I disembarked and walked across the tarmac, I felt the warm island air lick my face like a puppy

114

all over a master who has been away for a long time. It felt tangible, this air. Nice but suffocating. The truth is, I didn't really mind at all. I was not inclined to put up any resistance to this suffocating expression of love, so I simply gave in to the air's slurping tongue and its bark of welcome. I entered the terminal building and followed the passengers in front of me through the large glass doors. As I looked up, I saw scores of men, women and children pressed against the glass partitions on the upper level of the terminal, looking for their arrivals and waving to them. A woman in orange head-tie caught my eye, standing out like some warning signal.

At my turn at the customs checkpoint, I bid Mr. Simpson and his wife goodbye, shook their hands, and they both wished me an enjoyable stay. The customs officer, smugly cordial, checked my documents, stamping here, stamping there, and with a clipped smile told me to enjoy my stay. The loud but inaudible announcements coming through the intercoms and the groaning of the baggage conveyor-belts up ahead were making my head throb. In the baggage claim area, which teemed with people from other flights, a red-capped porter pounced on me, but I shook my head and pointed a finger towards the luggage check point ahead.

I was relieved to discover I was first in line. A tall male officer asked me if I had anything to declare. I said no; he stared disconcertingly at the camel hair jacket I wore.

'Open de bags there, man,' he said, in a slow rubbery accent. Head still throbbing, I took a little longer than normal to respond. The officer threw back his shoulders and stared at me with bulging eyeballs. I placed my carry-ons on the counter and unzipped the first bag. Before I had fully opened it, the officer's right hand descended roughly on the bag and began an irreverent rummage inside. After searching to his satisfaction, he hoisted back his shoulders again and in a brusque voice, tinged with contempt, said, 'Leh me see de next one.'

115

My insides swirled. Why was the man so rude? Who did he think he was talking to? I stiffened with anger and, ignoring his request, took up the bag whose contents were now in utter disarray, rearranged the crumpled shirts as best as I could, re-zipped the bag, and then deposited the other one on the counter. The officer carried out a similar, though briefer, assault.

'You can go on,' he said, looking away towards the line. 'Next!'

As I slung the bag over my shoulder and turned to leave, a casually-dressed white man walked forward. He was accompanied by a red-capped worker who carried three large suitcases on his cart. A few feet from the customs exit, I glanced back to see the same customs officer let this traveller through with a graceful, if obsequious, wave of the hand. So we stilled kissed-up to white people in this way. Had nothing changed?

A sour taste in my mouth, I left the terminal and walked through a large group of local people waiting to meet their parties. I spotted the orange head-tie again, and could now make out the face: round, unsmiling, worried-looking. I crossed a pavement and entered the taxi area. A horde of taxi drivers all seemed to have seen me at once and advanced like hunters with a net to trap me. I decided to focus on one cab and moved through the hailing hordes towards a blue and white taxicab. I placed my bags next to it and waited, keeping my eyes fastened before me. A short, brisk man wearing a green net shirt and dark gaberdine pants approached, took up the bags, and, without speaking, placed them in the trunk. I got in the front passenger seat. In a few seconds, we cruised out of the airport, and were soon on to what he called the ABC Highway.

'How much to Redman's Land?'

'Forty dollars.' It sounded an exorbitant amount. I looked around at the driver, whose entire body seemed to shake as he drove, as if he were moving to some imaginary music.

'You doan have to believe me, man. Look at this.' His body stopped moving. With his left hand, he flicked on the car's roof light, and I noticed the tyre-like bulge at the back of his neck. Using the same hand, he fished a folded and tattered sheet of paper from the glove compartment. Still looking straight ahead, he flattened out the document with a flick of the wrist.

'Take it,' he said, pushing the paper closer to me, like a slap in the face. Reluctantly, I took it. It carried a Barbados Government Printing Office stamp at the top and was spotted with what looked like coffee or tea stains. It verified that the forty-dollar fare from the airport to the city of Bridgetown was the government-regulated amount. I was silenced by my mistrust, but I didn't regret it.

'I know some guys doan go by this. But I do,' the taxi driver said with a victorious grin. He then replaced the tattered document and switched off the roof light all in one movement of his left arm. His voice was calmer now, almost intimate. 'I doan rip nuhbody off, yuh see. Dese fellas doan know that when duh rip people off duh does only frig-up themselves. Duh cyan guh back to that person and that person ain' going go back tuh dem.'

'This is my first visit back here in a long time. You hear things.'

'Sure. And some o'de tings yuh hear true too. But not me, man. I always play straight. You did in de States?'

'Yeah.'

'How long you did there?'

'Too long. Too long.'

'I supposin', too, you still t'inking in U.S. dollars, right?' He laughed, and I laughed with him. 'Forty Barbados dollars. Dat is wha' um is. Only twenty US. Cool so.'

With a combination of rebuke and humour, he had

lightened the mood, had drained the initial tension from the car. I had to admire him. I adjusted myself in the seat for greater comfort.

'What's the latest news in the country, man,' I asked. 'The fellow next to me in the plane said that Nelson statue was rearranged.' I laughed again, remembering that 'rearranged' was Geoffrey Simpson's word and that, when he said it, had suggested some painful plastic surgery.

'Yeah-man. It now facing de Careenage.'

'Was that somebody's idea of a joke? I know the man was a naval war hero and all that and looking seaward seems appropriate. But to go to all that trouble and expense just to turn him in a semicircle sounds pretty strange.'

'Strange? It more than strange. Is nothing but high-class foolishness. Dis blasted government doan know wuh de hell duh doing, man. You right. Dah is a good example of how duh wasting taxpayers' money 'bout dis place, man. Things in dis island dread dread dread, man. Dread.' The intimacy had left his voice. His words hammered with despair. 'A re-porter ask de Prime Minister what he vision is fuh de country and de Prime Minister (de Prime Minister!) look in de man face and say: "Vision is vision and action is action." But we goin' vote he to hell out this election. You tek um easy.'

'And you can't have an action plan without first having some vision of what the plan will be, right? Evasive. Very evasive.'

'Cha, man. Is foolishness. Nothing but high-class fool-ishness.'

'Vision is vision and action is action,' I repeated. 'Well, that's a new one to me, man.'

'I t'ink de Prime Minister trying he best, doan get me wrong. But he best far from good. We close-close to devaluation, you know, man. De man having meetings galore wid de IMF. Now, you know when a country got to go to the IMF, t'ings cyan be looking too good.'

'I thought Barbados was meant to be the flagship island now, economically...'

'Well, dat may be true, but how long you t'ink um going last if t'ings keep going like dis? De boss-man like he ain' able tuh negotiate loans out in de big countries. And why he doan tax de rich people higher? Is we poor people who catching de hell, you know, man. Not dem rich people. Raise de duties on new cars and other luxury goods. Why de hell he and he ministers cyan set de example fuh de country an' tek at least a twenty percent pay cut till t'ings straighten out? Dey cyan do dat? Cha.'

In the moonlight entering the car, I saw the driver's face had grown wet with perspiration. It was as if he had summoned the Prime Minister into the car and was addressing him rather than me. He sucked his teeth and shrugged his shoulders rapidly up and down. His body shook as if undergoing some allergic reaction. The Prime Minister's presence had disgusted him, and he had grown tired of it. He turned his head away from the PM and gazed steadily out the driver's window.

'Ah,' I said, concerned over the length of time he had taken his eyes off the road, 'but compared to Jamaica and Guyana (and even Trinidad), with all their natural resources, Barbados still has the strongest dollar, you must agree.'

To my relief, the driver turned his head and looked forward again. We approached a stop light at a cross roads.

'All dat may be true, Brother-man, but tell me how long um does tek to hit rock bottom once de IMF get duh claws 'pon yuh? Tell me dat?' He sucked his teeth again, for a much longer time, and shook his head from side to side. Little pools of saliva had gathered at the corners of his mouth.

'You're right,' I said, suddenly uncomfortable at the driver's intensity. 'You're absolutely right.'

119

We drove past several malls and commercial buildings, many of them, I noted, at least five storeys high. One complex housed a telecommunications network; another, an array of industrial buildings. When I left the island fifteen years ago, this kind of commercial activity was still relatively rare in the suburbs of Christ Church and the north-eastern parts of St. Michael. These areas were once exclusive neighbourhoods for White Barbadians. My old school friend, Christopher, later explained that as the older Whites died, many of their children sold the properties and went to live overseas. These properties were often purchased by local, White-owned real estate companies and developed for commercial use. These companies had also bought former plantation lands located in the parishes behind these areas, St. George and St. Phillip, and created housing developments for middle and upper class Blacks.

Everything seemed much larger than I remembered. The four-lane highway suggested progress of a kind. There had been no four-lane highways when I lived here. What I saw pleased me, but I also felt estranged, unable to identify anything intimately familiar. I had been raised here, had spent my first nineteen years here. I should have felt some sort of connectedness by now.

But as we turned on to Clapham Main Road, little tingles of familiarity began to encroach on my skin. My first sexual encounter had been with a Colombian-born girl named Aimey Romero who lived just off this road, through the gap in front of which I was now passing. I craned my neck out the window, but it was too dark to make out any details. I considered asking the driver to stop, but tiredness restrained me. I said nothing and reclined in my seat.

But how could I forget? Aimey's Barbadian brother-in-law, who lived with her family, was a music enthusiast. He had the most comprehensive collection of reggae and calypso records and cassette tapes of any one I knew, then or since. I used to go by the house at weekends to listen to music. One day in August, I remember Aimey standing on a chair putting up some curtains. I looked up and saw her thighs and crotch. The thighs were as smooth as sanded wood. She must have been about twenty then, two years older than I. I could not remember anyone else being at home. Had Aimey's brother-in-law, Stanley, gone to the shop or something? Were her younger brothers and sisters playing outside? Her mother at work? There had been no father. Stanley had met Aimey's sister when the cruise liner on which he worked berthed in Columbia's Puerto Estrella some ten years earlier. He had later sent for her. After they'd gotten married, the couple arranged for the rest of the Romeros to join them. But there had been no father. Aimey and I were alone at home that Saturday morning in August. After she had finished hanging the curtains that now slowly turned in the breeze, she left the room. Bob Marley was singing.

Darkness has covered my light
And changed my day to night.
Where is the love to be found?
Concrete jungle, where the living is hardest...

The Romeros, like many others in the neighbourhood, had a lot of mouths to feed. Stanley's work as a seaman was mostly seasonal. It was this music, this Caribbean blues, that kept us buoyant in the midst of hard times. In the background, I heard the sharp yapping of dogs. Next to me, the curtains continued their writhing dance.

Then I heard the shower running like a promise. Carrying the image of her sanded thighs, I entered the bathroom. Aimey didn't seem startled to see me. She merely threw back her jet-black, combed-out hair and continued lathering her body. Then she stepped under the spray. The rivering water wiped clean the suds from her tanned flesh. The passion she awakened left me speechless. She turned the tap off and reached for a towel. She never spoke a word. I reached over and held her before she wrapped herself, and she allowed the towel to drop back on to the rack. When I recognized her willingness, I suddenly let her go, as if I had embraced fire and eagerly, awkwardly, removed my clothes now damp from her body and embraced her again. I felt my body melt on her like wax.

The taxi careered down Clapham Hill and into Redman's Land. Every time we passed a street light, I craned my neck and scoured the area, but didn't try to make out every detail. I would have plenty of time for that in the days ahead. Now, I looked for larger landmarks. On the verges of Redman's Land, where once there had been a neighbourhood of chattel houses, a lower income government housing development erupted ablaze with light. That was new. Miss Wharton's shop still squatted at the corner of Sandbox Avenue and Redman's Main Road, just as I remembered it. As the car slowed down, I saw inside the shop. A couple of middle-aged women were buying groceries at the front counter. Two men, haloed by a brownish light, hunched in the background over a side counter specially erected for drinking men. Very rarely would a woman be seen at this side counter, unless she was a woman of questionable repute. I had seen this same scene so often, passing here as a teenager: men hunched over the side counter, firing shots of rum and leaving through the side door. It was a tradition. In the shop's back room, other men, with more time on their hands, would be drinking and playing cards, draughts, or dominoes. And sometimes sirens would be heard in response to a complaint about illegal gambling.

'Turn in here,' I said, pointing to the right and instructing the driver to take the second right turn on to Liverpool Road. 'Go right up to the cul-de-sac.'

At the dead-end, the car stopped and the driver switched off the ignition. A group of pariahs came howling out of the darkness and bared their teeth at the car. The driver got out, feigned throwing something at them, and they scampered off like demons into the dark. I got out, stretched, exhausted from the long journey. Then I walked slowly toward the back of the cab.

'Pot starvers,' the driver said as he removed the bags from the trunk of the car and handed them to me. I took the bags, paid and thanked him.

'Enjoy de stay, man,' he said. I nodded and turned towards the house. As I started walking along the driveway, I heard the cab setting off down the road, its noise gradually diminishing until it could no longer be heard. The bark of dogs was everywhere.

From what the crescent moon revealed, the house appeared the same as in the photographs. Halfway along the driveway, I found myself in the midst of knee-high grass and felt an army of burrs fastening like clenched teeth to my pants. I walked on to the front lawn area, which was also overgrown, though not as much as the driveway. The twin royal palms waved triumphantly at the star-spangled sky. I found the low front steps of the house and ascended them.

On the topmost step, I put down the bags and bent over to remove some burrs that had stitched themselves through my pants and were pricking my legs. Stiff from the flight, I pulled open the outer wrought-iron door. Then I bent over and fished a key from one of the bags. As I stood up, the key dropped from my hand and tinkled down the steps. I sighed hard, needled with fatigue. At last, the key found the lock on the front door, and I slipped into the pitch blackness of the house.

My right hand came up automatically to where I remembered the light switch used to be and found it. I hit the switch, but nothing happened. I turned the switch on and off several times with the same result. I fumbled for a box of matches in one of my bags and found too a plastic bag containing jasmine incense sticks. I had come prepared for a dusty, musty, smelly house, and I was not disappointed. I struck a match and the flame shot forth like a stunted, incandescent tail. It wagged, with me behind it, to a corner of the house where I found the breaker panel. I turned the breakers on and returned to the light switch just as the flame from the match died. I hit the switch again and this time a shock of bright yellow surrounded me: the yellow painted walls of the living room accentuated by the light. Suddenly, I found it difficult to breathe. The pent-up heat in the house and the lack of oxygen made me gag, so I lunged towards a front window and opened it. I opened a side window too and felt the warm relieving breezes rush over me like a salve. I took off my jacket but realized there was no chair or table to lay it on. Where had all the furniture gone? I hung the jacket on the window latch and looked around the room, in a state of growing anxiety. There was not a single piece of furniture in the living room, nor in the dining room, which could be seen from where I stood. Aunt Lolita hadn't said anything about selling or storing the furniture. I entered my parents' bedroom and struck the light switch. This room, too, stood empty. With an energy inspired by shock, I briskly entered the other two bedrooms. Empty! Empty! Into the kitchen. Empty! The entire house was a vacant shell. I forgot my tiredness and briskly moved around the house checking for any signs of a break-in. I finally gave up and stood there, leaning against the kitchen wall, thinking: *There is nothing*.

I thought of calling the police, but though Aunt Lolita had paid the service rates for water and electricity for the past year in anticipation of my arrival, she had discontinued the telephone service. It was eleven o'clock, so I couldn't ask a neighbour for a phone call so late in the evening. Besides, did the neighbours of my youth still live here? In the empty silence of the house my breathing sounded as if the earth itself was snorting, deeply, dolefully. I felt on the verge of a blackout because of the lightness in my head and leaned for support against the red-tiled cupboard that lined the left kitchen wall. I reached over to the sink and turned on the tap. Brownish fluid sputtered out and then flowed steadily. In half-a-minute or so, it cleared, and I cupped my right hand under the tap and sucked in some water. Then I threw generous amounts of the water onto my face using a shirt sleeve to wipe away the excess. I staggered into the living room, slid off my shoes, and made a pillow out of two towels. I found the floor and surrendered to sleep.

CHAPTER NINE

I awoke to what sounded like a tree's branch raking the galvanized roof or some giant termite eating the house. I grimaced at that thought and turned onto my left side towards the open front window. Still, pitch darkness outside. Despite the hardness of the pine floor, and a fleeting impressionistic dream about Elroy loudly wheeling through an unfamiliar house, I had managed a few hours of sound sleep. For this I was thankful. I had left on all the lights in the house. Now I turned away from the window and glanced at the Bulova on my wrist. It was ten minutes after five.

From where I lay, I could see through the archway (which separated the living and dining rooms), to the dining room and into part of the kitchen. Then I saw what looked like a small monkey hopping purposefully through the kitchen doorway. I jumped up. The thing, hearing my footsteps, halted in its tracks. Drawing closer, I soon realized it was a huge brown frog heading toward the back bedroom. I beat it to the bedroom door and stomped my right foot hard so that the creature flipped around like a wound-up toy and retreated towards the kitchen area. I continued stomping at strategic spots so that the frog hopped back through the doorway into the dining room. I outflanked it and tried to open the door in the dining room that lead outside. The door wouldn't budge. I went for my keys in the living room and returned to find the barnacled creature pressed into a corner like a school boy asked to face the wall for misbehaviour. With some difficulty, I opened the main side door and then the outer wrought iron door. Then I stomped the amphibian from its haven – and kept stomping until it made one graceless leap outside and landed awkwardly on the side step. I pulled at the door, but the wood had swollen and it wouldn't close, so I slammed it shut. Four cockroaches, like dried, windswept leaves, scurried down the wall and disappeared through a crack at its base.

I rubbed the slight soreness in my lower back, yawned and stretched, with my hands resting on the windowsill. I stuck my head outside to receive the cool morning air. Whistling frogs were still jamming as the sun crawled up behind the galvanized roofs and light glinted behind the waving ribs of coconut trees. A bus groaned along Redman's Main Road. A sheep bleated a ballad accompanied by the morning choir of crows, sparrows and doves. A cock's crow cracked the day wide open.

As the sunlight ate away the last crumbs of darkness, I took out an Almond Joy chocolate bar from one of my bags and, nibbling it, resumed my reverie at the window. *Give the neighbours time to wake*, I thought. *Then I'll go and ask to make a phone call*. Waist-high guinea grass and wild brush mottled with burrs now covered the neatly-trimmed front lawn of the photographs. The oleanders still flowered their poisonous pink asterisks, but had grown so tall they'd collapsed on top each other. But the twin royal palms still waved splendidly in the midst of this chaos of brush. Across the road, where the Johnsons used to live, a yellow and green brick house stood with the sign, *Elsee's Haircare*, projecting from it. Next to it, where the Grosvenors used to live, a huge tree stump rose from an open lot like an enormous rotting phallus.

I turned from the window, turned off all the lights and

went out of the back door and into the yard. It, too, was choked with bushes and high shrubs. It was still too early to call on my neighbours, so I began checking the condition of the outside back wall of the house. Everything seemed in good shape. Then I noticed a sign sticking out from behind the kitchen's iron waterpipe. Arced like a rainbow, its two ends curved in a ribboned design, the black sign carried the words 'GOOD HOPE' superimposed in white. My father had not lived to put it up.

I laid the sign on the back step and reluctantly pressed through the entangled overgrowth, knitted together in parts by cobwebs whose gossamer strands stuck in my hair and over my clothes. Medium-sized black and yellow spiders populated at least three of the webs. As I touched the strands, fluorescent backs scuttled deep into the protective greenery. My father's workshop, that had been partially hidden at the back of the yard, now appeared in front of me. A wild vine, whose roots resembled the legs of a centipede, held the broken door in position and almost completely covered it. I tore away as many of the vines as I could and felt the poisonous white juice trickle down my fingers. After wiping my hands in a patch of guinea grass, I entered the workshop. Various odds and ends cluttered it, making it difficult to find a way through. My father never refused anything offered to him; some day 'It would come in handy.' There were strewn pieces of chain, a tattered aluminium deck chair, cases of empty soda bottles (many of the bottles broken), a rusty garden spade, a machete, divers bits of iron pipe, rusted outdoor lamps with broken glass domes, pieces of deal wood and pine – all lengths. Brown termite trails lined the wood, and, in one corner of the roof, the termites' large globular nest stared down at me. But at the back of the workshop I found what I wanted, took up the hammer and nails and plied my way back through the bush. I nailed the sign over the front door and then headed down the road to where the Lashleys used to live. Instead of the gabled wooden house which I remembered, a white bungalow with black trimmings stood on the Lashleys' lot.

I opened the wrought iron gate and stepped onto the verandah. I thought of Mrs. Lashley's three older daughters – roughly my age – who had left the island for Brooklyn about the same time I left Barbados. Her younger children (I recalled there being three girls and two boys) had, as far as I knew, remained at home. I knocked on the door and a teenage girl, who distinctly resembled her mother, drew back the curtain and opened the glass door. From the back of the house, a dog bayed. The teenage Lashley greeted me with a coquettish smile. She wore a tightfitting floral cotton dress, and I could tell that she had become interested in boys. Tall and slender, hair styled with a fuzzy look. She glanced behind her to a curtained door space and shouted, 'Mum, someone hey!'

'Alphonso, Alphonso Hutson. An old neighbour of your mum. You know, I forget your name,' I said.

'Maureen.'

'Oh yes. Maureen. How're your other brothers and sisters?'

'They at work,' she said, rocking from side to side in a stationary dance.

Soon Mrs. Lashley waddled to the door. Maureen giggled 'Bye' and self-consciously walked through the curtained door space that led to the back of the house.

'Come in, Alph,' Mrs. Lashley said. 'Sit down, son. Wha' you is a big-able man now.' She carried a merry gleam on her face, although her plump swagger hinted at an aggressiveness brought on by hard experience. She wore a light green dress and looked just as I had remembered her except that the middle finger was missing from her right hand. Her hair hadn't even gone grey.

'Wha' how you? Man, I real glad to see you, yeh. When you get back?'

I told her. She offered me some breakfast which I gladly accepted: a cup of hot chocolate, a slice of coconut bread, and scrambled eggs. I inquired about her family and work. The girls in Brooklyn were doing fine. Maureen was the only child now still in school. Mr. Lashley had passed away a few years ago. She said she was doing all right, though, especially since most of the other children still living with her all had jobs and she still did shift work at the American-owned shoe factory. I thought, perhaps, that was where she had lost the finger, but didn't ask. The purpose of my visit loomed in my head, and Mrs. Lashley must have read my thoughts. She sat down in a caned mahogany chair and said, 'Man, I real glad to see you, yeh. You know, a few months ago you family, Verona and John, came with a truck and move out all the furnitures from de house. I did hoping and praying that you woulda come back. Man, I real glad to see you.'

'What you said, Mrs. Lashley? Verona and John Hutson did what? What I hearing at all? I hardly know them.'

'You mean, you nor you rich aunt didn' know 'bout dis?'

'Of course not. They're long-distanced relatives. Aunt Lolita told me they just surfaced when my parents died, looking to see what they could get. But she was here and they were wise enough not to mess with her. I came in last night and was wondering who took the things out the house.'

'Yes, man. They brought a big-able truck out here and clean out all the furnitures. Shoot. Like they fool evuhbody, 'causing duh seh you and you aunt turn things over to them. 'Causing they is Hutsons, evuhbody believe them. And wid you out so long, nuhbody t'ink you int'rested in de place.'

'What the France I hearing at all?'

'Well, they got evuht'ing. I ain' get not even a light bulb. Anything so, I know your nice mum and your nice dad woulda gih we something. We used to live real good, yuh know?'

'True, Mrs. Lashley,' I said, bristling with rage. I started to pace. After all these years of prevarication, I had finally summoned enough courage to confront my past, and here were these two people, whom I hardly knew, seemingly bent on complicating my mission.

'This is very serious,' I said, passing a hand across my head. 'I only here for a few weeks and don't have time for all this madness. I have to do this the right way before I kill somebody and get myself in trouble.'

'Alph, doan talk like that,' Mrs. Lashley said. 'But I understand how you feel.'

'Don't they have any respect for people's family traditions? Could I use your phone, Mrs. Lashley?'

'Sure, Alph. You know you doan even have to ask.'

During the hour it took for the police to arrive, I called Simone collect to let her know I had arrived safely in the island. She said the girls missed me but ventured no further conversation. For this I was grateful. I didn't feel like talking about my parents' house. I asked to speak to Denise and Lucinda and told them I loved them.

After I hung up, Mrs. Lashley and I went onto the verandah to watch for the police jeep. When I saw it approaching, I walked up the road and met the police at the house. They searched for forced entry and found none. On our way outside, I realised that the front wrought iron door had not been padlocked as the side one had been. I had been so tired when I arrived, I hadn't noticed this. Someone, John probably, must have cut off the padlock and either picked the front door lock to get inside the house or taken off the door lock to have keys made and then replaced it. The thieves had used the front entrance exclusively, it seemed.

'There are two people who were seen gaining access to this house, Officers: Verona and John Hutson. I'd appreciate it if you'd accompany me to their homes to see if the furniture's there.'

The officers glanced at each other several times.

'They are family to you?' one of them asked.

'Yes. But I didn't give them permission to come in here. They broke the padlock to get in here. I have a witness to prove they came and stole the things. They're the only two people who could've gotten in here.'

'Dis sound like a family matter,' the other officer said.

'Please. Could you go with me, sir. I don't have much time in the island and, if the things are there, it'd be easy enough just to get them returned.'

They walked over to the driveway to confer. I remained standing on the steps. After a few minutes, they joined me and reluctantly agreed to accompany me. I found the addresses in an old telephone directory that was lying on top of a pile of old newspapers. The officers already had gotten in the jeep by the time I came outside again. As we passed her house, Mrs. Lashley, looking solemn, waved to us from her verandah.

Twenty-five minutes later, we turned off the main road in St. George, and went down a small hill that levelled out near an unpainted rum shop. I asked the policeman to reverse the vehicle so I could ask the shopkeeper where to find Verona Hutson's house. The telephone directory had listed no house number. I hopped out the jeep and entered the shop and got directions. We drove for another two hundred yards before we arrived at Verona's, an unpainted, rickety, wooden building squatting on bricks placed strategically underneath it for support. Mildewed coral stones, the largest at the bottom and the smallest at the top, made up the front steps. Nearby, a pariah sounded as if it were baying for blood.

'You stay here,' one of the officers said. Craning backwards, I watched the two policemen ascend the coral steps. The door was open halfway and, after a lengthy pause, they went inside. I looked through the passenger window of the jeep and across the asphalt that shimmered with heat. Even from within the vehicle the glare made me squint. A bald, elderly man came out from the yard of a nearby chattel house, painted aquamarine. He wore a vest and brown shorts and carried a water bucket. He came around to the front of the house and, bending down, repeatedly scooped out water from the bucket with his hand into a hedge of crotons. A brown, common-breed dog, tongue lolling, came up to him. A young man riding a bicycle cut across the scene, and the dog began a fierce yapping, following the cyclist right up to the road. Its mustard coloured coat reminded me of my father's dog, Bronze. Then, tongue lolling again, the mutt turned and disappeared behind the house.

I heard an insistent clapping of hands and turned around. Looking through the jeep's back window, I saw one of the officers beckoning. I opened the door and leapt out the jeep, but, as I approached the house, apprehension started growing and I slowed my pace. Suppose the things weren't there? Suppose Verona had cunningly stored them at a friend's or neighbour's? What I hoped I would have going for me was the element of surprise. Yet, I couldn't even be sure of that. What if Verona had been smart enough to secure allegiances among some residents of Liverpool Road? What if one of them had seen me arrive last night and had forewarned her? What would I do then? John Hutson would be the next stop. It would take at least half an hour to get to his house. Wouldn't Verona call him immediately after I had left her house to tip him off? Wouldn't he then make sure that no one was at his house when I arrived?

I entered the house. Verona had been cooking. The pungent odour of onions and cornmeal greeted me. She stood in the hallway, arms akimbo, her face set like stone, defiant and stubborn – although (for the brief moment our eyes made contact) I thought I glimpsed fear run over her long ebony face. She must have been in her sixties. I didn't speak to her. I resolved to remain undistracted by her angry glares. My chief concern was to ascertain whether or not my family's belongings were somewhere in this house.

'Can I go in the bedroom?' I asked one of the officers, who nodded in response. Both officers looked expectant, as if they were anticipating some more explicit confrontation.

I pushed open the bedroom door. Just one step inside, and I could go no further. Stacks of furniture, like wooden hills, made the room virtually impassable. I squeezed myself in to start to identify them: my parents' mahogany glassware cabinet and the set of four caned mahogany chairs; the leaf-green sofa and matching chairs which they had gotten from the Simpsons; my parents' bed frame leaning against the wall; my wrought-iron folding bed; a wrought-iron dining table and four matching chairs; a white wrought-iron telephone table; a wooden glassware cabinet; a large vinyl-covered book case. These items had been crammed into the room with Verona's own bedroom furniture. I was at once surprised and relieved.

'Officers!'

They came to the bedroom door.

'These are the things,' I said. We searched the kitchen and the other bedroom of this four-room chattel. More of my belongings filled the second bedroom: another wooden cabinet containing British-made blue china vases and tea sets given to my mother by the Simpsons; another bed; a caned mahogany divan; my mother's combination wardrobe and vanity set. The television set, fridge, gas stove, stereo and all the albums and cassettes were nowhere to be found. We returned to the living room to find Verona seated in a caned mahogany chair, humming what sounded like a hymn and nodding her head.

'I doan know netting 'bout dum,' she said defiantly when I inquired about the missing items. Her short frame quivered with rage or disappointment or fear. 'Your Aunt gave me keys to get in the house, and I didn' see no t.v., fridge, stove nor netting else.' She fixed her head in front of her as if she were addressing the floor. Under her right eye, a large mole, from which a tuft of hair protruded, quivered as she spat out the words and then thrust herself backward in her seat.

'My aunt didn't tell me anything about that,' I said roughly. 'The house was secure enough. You're a liar!' But I knew I couldn't win. I only had a few weeks in the island, and with Aunt Lolita in New York, how could I prosecute her? In response, Verona started to rock backwards and forwards as if in a rocking chair, her eyes averted, her bowed spider legs clawing at the floor.

'You see what I said,' began the doubtful constable. 'Dis sound like a family thing to me.'

Suddenly, Verona burst out, 'But, Alphonso, you really t'ink you shoulda do this to me? We is family...'

'I hardly know you,' I said. 'This is the second time in my life I've ever seen you.'

'...bringing de police hey so sudden on me to raise my pressure. All you had to do wus call me and we woulda straighten t'ings out. I got dese t'ings in here 'cause you aunt tell me she wus leaving fuh de States and she didn' want to leave de t'ings in de house wid all de vandalism goin' on 'bout de place. So why de ass you troublin' me for, nuh? Look, de first chance yuh get, come and tek dese blasted t'ings outta my place, hear!'

'A family affair,' the constable said, in a voice full of grief for getting involved. I desperately tried to hold on to myself. I knew Verona was lying. Aunt Lolita was too meticulous,

135

too much the perfectionist, not to have told me if such arrangements had been made. Verona was shrewd. In Aunt Lolita's absence, it was my word against hers, and I didn't have time to take the matter to court.

'You can holler as loud as you like,' I said. 'Tomorrow, I'm coming to get these things that you stole. You're a thief. These officers here are my witnesses, so see and be here.'

Accompanied by a volley of Verona's spitting invective, I marched across the room toward the door. The two officers followed.

'Tek um easy, mums,' I heard one of them say.

Inside the jeep, I threw myself down on the seat, fluttering with rage, but grateful that my family's furniture, at least most of it, had been found.

It rained all afternoon and part of the night. Next morning, Mrs. Lashley gave me the name of a Mr. Carrington who rented trucks and cars. I called him and, around lunchtime, a dreadlocked youth showed up in an open-back truck. Mrs. Lashley's late husband had worked for Mr. Carrington for over twenty years, and she had maintained contact with the company. I had requested a half-dozen cardboard cartons, and I could see their tops rising from the back of the truck.

'I's Mr. Carrington main man. De man name Ishi,' the Rastafarian said as I got into the truck. I was immediately struck by Ishi's massive frame. Although he was sitting, I could tell he would be well over six feet tall. He wore an oversized plaid shirt, blue jeans, and black shoe-boots of the kind that had steel tips. Even with his uneven beard and the Medusa-like locks, a softness, a calmness, emanated from him. This softness did not smack of anything effeminate. Rather, it seemed to be the softness of a kindly spirit coupled with a calmness born of discipline. It would take a lot to ruffle him. Ishi said that when we returned and off-loaded the furniture, he'd drive me over to his workplace so

I could collect the rented car. Mr. Carrington had told him we could do all the paperwork then.

Around two o'clock, we arrived at Verona's. The heavy rain had sucked up some of the heat from the earth. What was left, moist and fetid, coiled around houses, traffic, people. This wasn't the humidity of midsummer Georgia or Louisiana. It was a moister, denser humidity. Days of sustained rain were needed to suck out more of the heat and bring cooling.

Ishi and I wrapped all the glassware and china in old newspapers and packed them in the cardboard boxes. We loaded the heavier items onto the truck first and stacked the glassware on top of them. It took about two hours to complete all the packing and loading. When we were finished, I left Ishi on the truck securing the taller objects so they would not fall over and bump against each other. Then I re-entered the house to make sure I'd taken everything. Inside the second bedroom, I noticed a mahogany leg projecting out of the closet. I opened the closet door wider and removed my mother's antique night chair. The basin was missing. On my way out with this last item, I passed Verona seated in the same chair as before. She was rocking backwards and forwards.

'Well, looka you,' she said. 'You is a real Hutson, though.' She giggled with a cackling sound. I stopped and turned to face her. 'Man, you is a real Hutson,' she repeated. What did she mean? That the Hutsons didn't let anybody walk over them? Were warmongers? Were hard on each other? It was difficult to pin down her tone, difficult to know whether behind the laughter lay sarcasm or admiration or pure cunning.

'But, look,' she continued, the bowed spider legs wriggling under her, 'you come hey to de island after all dese 'ears and ain' bring me netting. Not a red cent.' Her bloodshot eyes laughed more than ever. 'Wha' loss!' she cried, raising both hands in the air as one rejected. She let her hands fall down on her lap. 'Wuh yuh cyan gimme a few o' dem cups and glasses that yuh got in de mahog'ny cab'net?'

I thought, *This is enough. This is too much.* It seemed as though a demon writhed behind the black mask of her face. I felt sick to my stomach. I stood, with the night chair in my hand, staring at her and feeling disgust growing inside me. I found myself struggling to determine if I should knock her away like a spider, laugh, or simply flee.

'You know, John is de body who arrange all this, yuh know. Net me.' She kept moving her hands and feet as she spoke, a giant black spider in a worn brown dress. The hairy mole on her face wriggled and crinkled like a sniffling snout. 'I doan know how he do um, but he got copies o' de title deed to de propurty. But I ent had netting to do wid netting. I real sorry now I tried to help out you aunt by tekking all dese t'ings in here.'

'I see. So you were to get the contents and John the house?' I said in a low voice. 'That was the plan, wasn't it? I guess you've sold off the other things that missing. Easy cash, eh?'

My right hand, in which I held the night chair, twitched.

'People like you and John want locking up. I have five minds to get both of you locked to hell up. You all lucky I'm only here for a few weeks. Lucky as hell. What's the name of the damn lawyer, Verona?'

'I dunno.' She pushed her head coyly up in the air. 'Ask John. He would know.'

I detected sarcasm in her voice and felt my hand tighten around the night chair. I felt my hand rising. Suddenly, from behind Verona, two figures started to form. As they got clearer, I recognized the faces of my parents. My father raised his right hand with frantic upward-outward movements that indicated he wanted me to leave. He shouted, 'No! No!' but no sound came out. I could tell what he was saying from reading his lips. My mother put an arm around him and started to cry. I felt the night chair lower in my hand, and I turned to leave the house.

Just then I heard a man's voice. It wasn't my father nor was it Ishi. I spun around and saw someone in a wheelchair wheeling rapidly down the hallway in my direction. The wheels thundered over the pine floor. Verona had gotten up and was slowly walking towards the back of the house. She stood between me and the figure in the wheelchair. As the wheelchair came to a stop, Elroy, face contorted like a gargoyle's, said, 'Don' 'serve live. Don' 'serve live.'

Don't deserve to live. She don't deserve to live. I raised the night chair again, this time with both hands, and went after her. She heard my approach and spun around. I saw the terror in her eyes, the panic. But I was too quick. Concentrating on her fear, I wanted to witness her pain the moment the chair made contact with her head. What I didn't realize was that my father had returned. All I saw was an outstretched hand pushing the chair to one side as it made its descent. The night chair crashed on to the floor, breaking two of its legs and sending splinters everywhere.

'Murder! Murder! Murder!' Verona screamed and clasped her head with both hands. 'O God! O God! Murder!' Seconds later, I heard loud knocks at the door. Verona, still holding her head, now drooped as if she would fall. She stumbled, knockkneed, through the house, pushed open the front door and went outside. I calmly gathered some of the splinters of my past.

'Verona, you awright?' I heard one female voice say.

'Wha' happen? Wha' happen?' asked another.

I came outside and stood on the front steps. At least fifteen people, mostly women, but a few men and children as well, pressed around Verona. She sat on the bottommost step, hunched and sobbing fitfully. One woman fanned her; another produced a glass of water. They all looked up at me with slicing, questioning looks.

139

'I t'ink I better call de police,' a gruff voice said. It was the bald-headed man with the crotons and the mutt.

'Doan worry wid dat,' Verona said and put a hand to her throat as if it pained her to speak. 'Dis is de son o' my late husband cousin. He hey from de States.'

I slowly walked down the steps. Ishi had gotten out of the vehicle and stood by the roadside beckoning me to hurry up. I hadn't thought I would ever see him lose his composure. It was as if he had given it to me, and I was bursting at the seams with both his confidence and mine. I smiled and hailed him. In spite of the still scowling neighbours, I felt a curious uplift. And this feeling of triumph lay in the knowledge that Verona knew the exact nature of my victory. That's why she wouldn't let the man call the police. It was only she and I in the house, when, with blood on my mind, I had raised the night chair. Her word against mine. Now, we were even. Suddenly, as one taken by surprise, I raised both hands and stared at them. Then my hands started to shake, and I broke out in a profuse sweat. My heart rate accelerated and then a feeling of listless enervation swept over me. I felt I would blackout at any minute as I collapsed onto the passenger seat. The reality of what had just transpired was before me now, sweeping over me like a gusty wind agitating sugar cane fronds. I kept thinking that I could have killed her. Just like that, in the heat of a moment, I could have been a murderer. 'Oh my God!' I kept saying again and again, repeatedly looking at Ishi and at my hands. 'What happened back there? I can't believe I almost hit her with the chair…' Oh Elroy. Who was he? What was he?

Around six o'clock, we off-loaded the furniture. Since I intended to rent the house unfurnished, we stacked all the items in the third bedroom. I asked Ishi about the car. He said that since business was now closed, he'd bring it for me in the morning. I gave him a twenty-dollar tip, the largest I'd ever given anyone, and went inside for a shower.

Early next morning, I called John Hutson from Mrs. Lashley's. His brusque tone indicated he had already been briefed.

'You go to Ron Hewitt. Do what I tell you. I have nothing more to say. See de lawyer Ron Hewitt and come and get the key to the house. And, besides, I have this whole conversation on tape. I have all I need to have on tape.'

'You can't intimidate me, you fool. Don't you have any kind of respect? Who gave you the right to try to acquire this property? I could put you in serious legal trouble, you don't know that?'

'Come and get this key, you hear? Come and get this key,' he kept repeating.

'The truth is, your plans backfired in your nasty face,' I said. 'You'll never be a landlord now; at least, not with this property. Everyone sees you as a respectable social worker, but I know better. You're nothing but a cheap nasty thief, a filthy grave robber.' I hung up the phone and went home to wait for Ishi who arrived just after eight in a blue Suzuki. I took him back to Carrington's Truck and Auto Services and completed all the necessary paper work.

Before going into Bridgetown to retrieve the copy of the title deed, I drove over to collect the key from John Hutson. I pulled up on the driveway of his cream coral-stone bungalow in a middle-class suburb called Wildey Terrace. A plump young woman with an unhappy-looking face and staring eyes appeared. I presumed she was John's daughter. When I asked to speak to him, she said stiffly that he wasn't there and handed me a key. Then she quickly closed the door.

CHAPTER TEN

I left Ron Hewitt's office and stood on the pavement on one side of Spry Street. Elroy was with me. He clung to my skin like the heat leaping off the asphalt and the glare that made me squint. Whenever possible, I walked in the shade and shaded my eyes with a hand to escape his incessant prod. It was as if he was saying, 'Deal with me. Deal with me. Don't ignore me any more.' How much longer could I put off our fraternal embrace? I glanced at my watch. Eleven forty-five. An elderly woman wearing a straw hat walked slowly along the road in the direction of Roebuck Street. Almost bent in half, she held a straw basket over one arm. It was as if some unnameable burden weighed her down that had nothing to do with the basket she carried. My eyes followed her, and I thought of my mother who would have been about her age had she lived. Early seventies or so. A tall youth with spectacles approached and passed in front me. He wore a white shirt with the long sleeves rolled up, the two top buttons undone. In spite of the casual dress, there was something formal about him. A clerk in one of the government departments who had decided to take off his tie and make himself comfortable on his lunch break? On the other side of the road, a wooden blue and pink building housed a real estate office. Chains ran alongside it and connected to the Cathedral's wall, enclosing a small parking lot guarded by a man in a little wooden hut.

I made a right turn along Spry Street in the opposite direction to the old woman. I passed a boutique, a hair salon, and a buildings supplies office before gaining St. Michael's Row. The sun crashed down on my neck and arms. I felt the heat from the road pushing through my tennis shoes. The city traffic was thick where St. Michael's Row met Bridge Street: cars and heavy duty vehicles, workers on their lunch breaks, tourists, and senior citizens making their way to the bus terminals. At the intersection of Palmetto and Bridge streets, a fruit vendor loudly chanted: 'Aw-ring-ges! Ju-see aw-ring-ges!' A blue and white minibus, with the words 'Road Warrior' on its side, pulled dangerously around the Palmetto Street corner. The loud bass of dub music leapt out its windows.

I passed a set of colonial-style government buildings and began thinking about the documents I had retrieved from the lawyer. I felt relieved, but I knew I had greater challenges before me. I hadn't even begun to tackle the forces that had tugged me to the island. The missing furniture had not been in my original plans, but it seemed now to have brought me closer to the residue of my past. My parents and Elroy had visited me as I hovered over Verona with the night chair, but I hadn't visited them yet, hadn't seen their graves or said goodbye. I wanted to visit them, and I didn't want to visit them. Something raked long and hard inside me, and my mind found refuge on the steps of GOOD HOPE. I felt safe there.

I had decided on tenants rather than selling the house. Mrs. Lashley had insisted on finding a tenant for me. She said that my nice mum and nice dad wouldn't have approved of me selling the property and that she knew a young, recently-married couple who might be interested. The couple, it turned out, were very interested. They were members of Mrs. Lashley's apostolic church. The house was very conveniently located for them.

143

I reached Broad Street. Inside the Cave Shepherd department store, the air conditioner rescued me from a headache brought on by the heat. I took the escalator to the second floor and ate lunch in the restaurant overlooking the street.

At one-thirty, I left Cave Shepherd and headed for my rented car parked off Coleridge Street. On my way to it I saw a sign on a building: CHRISTOPHER RILEY PROPERTY MANAGEMENT CONSULTANTS. This had to be my old school buddy, Christopher Riley. I would call in to arrange a meeting with him before leaving the island. I felt a curious uplift at the thought that I might have finally matched him socially and economically. I entered the building, excited at the prospect of seeing my old friend and also by the knowledge that he was in a business whose services I needed.

Christopher wasn't in the office, the secretary told me. Slim, young, fair-skinned. Had anything changed? I made an appointment for nine o'clock the following day, Thursday. I had two weeks left before returning to the U.S., and it seemed everything was falling into place. But when I went to see Christopher the next day, the secretary said he wasn't in his office, that he had come to work but had left again for an appointment.

'But I had an appointment with him,' I said.

'Well,' the young woman said, 'he's out, and I don't know how long Mr. Riley is going to be. Could you check back this afternoon, please?'

I left, my head ringing with frustration. I thought about going to find where Elroy rested, where my parents rested. They were more important than the house. I wondered whether my remorse over not attending my parents' funeral had made me feel I didn't deserve the house and this was another reason why I had no problem in letting Aunt Lolita take charge of it.

What I found myself doing was browsing in various

music stores and sampling their ranges of acoustic guitars. Then I went to Cave Shepherd, bought some clothes, a double-burner hotplate, and a small cooler. Before going upstairs to the restaurant, I stopped in the record room to buy some local music. The attendant, a young man with fashionably oversized clothes, was patient with me. Nothing he played interested me until he put on Gabby's 'Across the Board'. I was struck by the cover of the album which showed the calypsonian in an African print fingering an acoustic Gibson Epiphone, the same guitar I now owned. The album had been released several years ago and some of the lyrics dealt with topical issues which I didn't understand. Some days later over lunch, Christopher explained that the song, 'Chicken and Ram', had to do with a Barbados-based Trinidadian business woman who had dumped unsanitary chicken on the Barbados market, and that 'The List', told the story of a homosexual who, before dying of AIDS, had made a list of the names of men he had slept with. Many of the people on the list were politicians and other high ranking men.

I bought the album, ate lunch, and, from the pay phone at the store, called Christopher's office. For five minutes I held the line. When the secretary returned, she said Christopher was still occupied on another line and that I would have to call him back. When I did, Christopher had left the office 'for an urgent meeting', the secretary said. It took three more days before I was able to see him.

With just a week left in the island, the secretary finally ushered me into Christopher's office. At each end of his desk, were piles, each about a foot high, of neatly-stacked files. I saw the hills of files before I saw him and behind them he appeared much shorter than I remembered. But there he was, in a beige shirt jack, looking up from between them. He looked intense. Where was the broad boyish smile lighting up the round face that I remembered? Now, his thick moustache and the peak of his beard were flecked with gray. Head leaning diagonally, a black telephone locked between his right shoulder and ear, Christopher acknowledged me with a glance and a slight nod.

'What did he say? That we're destabilizing Barbados? That our confrontational tactics will run out the tourists? That's the typical scare-tactics those bastards always use. Every time Black people resist exploitation, they're labelled as subversives.' There was a long response from the other end of the line. Then Christopher said, 'Anyway, Ryan, I got to go. I have someone in my office. I'll have the files sent over, and I'll see you Saturday at the meeting.'

Christopher hung up the phone and looked directly at me, at once surprised and contemplative.

'Alphonso, man, it's good to see you. How're things? I haven't seen you since high school.' His broad smile reclaimed my memory of him. He rocked backwards in his brown swivel chair, then caught himself and reached over the desk with his right arm outstretched. 'You still living?' he asked, giving my hand a firm shake and then quickly letting it go.

'Good to see you too, Christopher,' I said, glancing around the office. Framed certificates mottled the gray walls, and a pencil print of a woman, holding a water pot on her head with one hand and the hand of a chubby child with the other, hung almost directly over Christopher's head. On top of a grey filing cabinet, a low male voice spilled from a red transistor radio.

'You seem to be doing pretty well for yourself,' I said. 'Gorgeous personal secretary. It's good to see the old fellas doing well. How's your father?'

Christopher sat back in his chair and looked as though he was studying me. He rubbed his right forefinger slowly over his moustache; his expression told me his mind was somewhere else.

146

'Still there,' he said, adjusting himself and folding his arms. 'Retired and still chasing after all the young girls. You should go and give him a look-up. But the old lady passed away two years ago.'

'Sorry to hear, man. You heard I lost both my parents to a car accident?'

'That's rough, man. I heard something 'bout that. I was up in England doing some studying, I think. Came back here 'bout ten years ago. Wasn't going anywhere working my ass off for the sons of planters. So, five years ago, I decided to stop working for other people. So here I am. It's a struggle, though.'

'Struggle?'

'I could use some business, man. You think it's easy for a Black businessman round here? So, tell me, you got some business for me?' Christopher said this in jest, for he had no idea how pertinent his question was.

'You think you could see after my parents' house for me? It's still there in Redman's Land...'

'See after it? Don't make sport, my friend. Joan'll take care of everything. Tenants?'

'Yeah,' I said pleased at my good fortune. 'So you think Mr. Riley'll remember me after all this time?'

'Of course. You look the same way. A little bit more size, that's all. How long you in the island for?'

'Another week or so. We'll see how things go. If I don't see him this time, I'll check him out when I come back.'

'And when will that be, Alphonso? Another sixteen years?' Christopher had gotten serious again. He shook his head from side to side. 'All our best brains overseas.' He straightened up in the chair and continued, 'You know that fella Ryan I was talking to on the phone when you came in? Ryan Proute. The head of the Barbados Workers Party. Now, that's a man committed to this country. He could've lived anywhere in the world, but he chose to remain here.

147

It's a new party and we aim to win the elections next month. I'm one of his advisers. I'm not a member of the executive, but I advise him privately. We're good friends. That man is a symbol of commitment.'

'You need a godfather to make it on this island, Christopher. And *that* I didn't have. But tell me,' I said, paddling clear of the commitment rocks. 'Mr. Riley still driving that white Peugeot?'

'You better believe it, man,' Christopher said, looking at me, yet seeming to stare through me. He gave the impression that something was going on behind his words, as if they masked some other emotion, some other desire. 'The old man's stubborn as hell. Even with the crazy costs of maintaining a car like that, he still won't consider a newer model.'

'They don't build cars like that any more, Christopher.'

'The costs ain' worth it, man. With the amount of money he pours into that guzzler, he could've purchased a few new cars by now.'

The intercom sounded. Christopher took up the receiver and told Joan to hold his calls.

'I'm glad to see you back in the island, Alphonso. And I hope you'll consider staying, though I guess, by now, you have a family, yes?'

'Yeah. Two daughters. Things ain' too good with the wife right now, though. We're just about separated. And you?'

'Still single. I don't know if I'm cut out for marriage. But right now, that's the last thing on my mind. But you could say I'm wedded to this country. Call what I'm saying pretentious crap, if you like, but I'm dead serious. Come to our meeting Saturday morning and see what we're up to. We could use someone like you.'

'We?'

'Yes, my movement, The Alliance for Economic Democracy. We ain' no political party. Just concerned Barbadians. Concerned that in spite of the '37 riots, in spite of the

Mutual Affair in '88, the minority still controls this economy. They're the real rulers of this country, and that's not right. This November, we'll celebrate thirty years of independence. What are we celebrating? Political governance without economic control is meaningless. Until we control those resources, we can never be independent.'

This was Christopher speaking with an eloquence and seriousness I had never associated with him. To me, he was a rich man's son who had been fond of me. But he was never a brilliant scholar. He simply got by. There had been something nonchalant about him. This new passion surprised and drew me.

'I know of the '37 riots, how they deported Clement Payne, but what was the Mutual Affair?'

'Don't you know that for three hours during those same riots, a large group of Bajans put the Mutual Building under siege? The same Mutual Building of the Mutual Affair. Quite a coincidence, isn't it? Black insurance policy holders challenged the Mutual's management, demanding they place democratically elected Black directors on the Board. The Mutual management's reaction was predictable. They said we were motivated by racism. What a joke. Listen. If we preached about racism, then they practised it, yes? I was one of those young policy holders, Alphonso. Our leader, Harcourt Hilary, made a big impression on me. He awakened me, a professional Black Bajan, to an appreciation of what it really meant to stand up for my rights. I soon found myself a frontrunner in this bid for change and one of the five candidates nominated by the policy holders as directors to the Mutual's Board.'

Christopher told me how he'd returned to Barbados in 1988, planning to work for a big corporation, to move up in the company, become an executive, make a good living. With a good degree, in a country whose population was mostly Black like him, these should have been realizable goals, but when he'd joined the accounting department of the Barbados Shipping and Trading as a junior accounts clerk (thanks to his father's contacts), he'd watched as White junior clerks, hired after him, and often relying on him to get their accounts out of sticky situations were given bigger salary increases and promotions. Even the managers came to him with accounting problems they couldn't solve. Many of these lacked qualifications for their positions, but had gotten their jobs through family connections. After two years, he hadn't moved anywhere in the company, so he'd decided he could make it on his own.

Christopher said he was by then no longer the naive son of a retired government meteorologist. Blacks could progress in the civil service, and if that were the extent of their ambitions, they could have a stable, decent middle-class life. But in private enterprise, unless you were prepared to do everything on the terms of the White employers there were only brick walls.

It was his experience in Barbados Shipping and Trading – one of the many companies The Mutual had large investments in – that had led him to involvement in the Mutual Affair.

Christopher vividly recalled the day of the meeting, how he'd walked with Harcourt and two other nominees up the coral steps of the Mutual building filled with a sense of destiny, how Harcourt had seemed extraordinarily calm, though he was being labelled a communist and receiving regular death threats, how the Board Room pulsed from wall to wall with over two hundred bodies and the six suited Mutual Board members sat with stolid expressions, staring ahead, stony as statues, at a sea of Black faces. My ears pricked up when Christopher mentioned Geoffrey Simpson's name; he was the Board's Chairman.

Harcourt had got up to describe the Mutual's authority structure as no different from that of an old-style slave

150

plantation. The only other sound in the room, Christopher said, was the breathing of the determined body of Black policy holders, faces transfixed, gleaming with a mixture of disbelief and triumph that one of their own was challenging three hundred years of power. The faces of the Board members were flushed or steeled with a grim determination. Then Geoffrey Simpson stood up, introduced himself and stiffly invited questions from the floor.

When it came time for nominations, Christopher said, they'd been tactically naive by nominating all five of the Alliance's members to the board. Geoffrey Simpson had announced that, as it was running late, the election of directors would be held the following Friday during the Mutual's Annual General Meeting.

In the days which followed, very different responses from the public flooded the airwaves. On the one hand, Harcourt's critics denounced him for being crudely aggressive; on the other, supporters praised him for pursuing the dream of economic liberation and democracy in the island. As the week wore on, Christopher had become increasingly concerned that they were fielding too many candidates. They all knew if only one of them ran, it would have to be Harcourt. That left four. They agreed that Patsy Trotman should also run, to articulate the concerns of the women policy holders. But then the remaining three each felt they had the right to run. Was this selfishness? An inability to understand the implications of their decisions, when the only chance lay in sacrifice, in denial of personal satisfaction? For eight years, Christopher said, he'd pondered these questions. There had been another element that sealed their defeat. Although they represented the interests of the Black middle-class, they received little support from that group. They, too, labelled them communists and subversives. On election day, old and infirm Whites found their way to the polling booth, but the majority of able-bodied Black policy holders stayed at home.

The Mutual's incumbents retained their positions, re-tained their two token Black directors and Christopher's group failed to get any progressive Black persons onto the board. They succeeded, though, in raising the conscious-ness of many to the continuing lack of democracy and racial equality in the island's economic structures. They began to see what had happened as preparation for a larger fight to democratize the economic resources of the entire island, but they recognized they would need the support of sections, at least, of the Black middle class.

'I saw this as a war, Alphonso. It was a war. Them and us. More precisely, them and them, and us. The second "them", the Black middle class. How to win? We saw that people who hold power don't let it go for a joke, man. You got to find other ways to dismantle power.'

'What was your solution?'

'In '91, I formed the Alliance for Economic Democracy. So you see now why you had such a hard time getting hold of me? Elections coming up next month. My organization has a role to play. We're advising the BWP. We hope they'll win. We're in the middle of another revolutionary period, Alphonso. We see this as the final initiative: the democrati-zation of resource control in this island. This time, we intend to win the war.'

CHAPTER ELEVEN

It was time to pay Clarence Brown a visit. On my way there on Friday evening, I thought about what Christopher had said and how he had imparted to me an enthusiasm for the island that I thought I'd long ago lost. For the first time in a long while, I felt the possibility of belonging and found myself anxiously looking forward to Saturday and Christopher's meeting. Clarence, by contrast, had been the one who encouraged me to leave the island. He'd been frustrated and disappointed with Barbados and saw no hope for himself, though I'm sure he encouraged me to leave out of genuine concern for my welfare. With or without Clarence's negative portrait of the island, I'd wanted to leave. I didn't have a family to get me a good job as Christopher's had done. But now, on the way to see Clarence, what did I really feel? Were the feelings that Christopher had stirred in me just sentimental yearnings for home? Yet, if I was finally on my native earth, finally in the hallways of my immediate ancestors, why had I not gone to touch the ancestral gravestone and that black wooden cross? They had spoken to me, voicelessly, had prevented me from possibly murdering someone, just as Elroy had wheeled my guilt and deepest fears, pounced and stuck to my skin. *Deal with me. Deal with me. Don't ignore me any more.* But, just as I'd pursued contact with Christopher instead of tasting my dead blood, I had to see Clarence if he was around.

153

I had been so apprehensive about my visit to Barbados that I hadn't even thought to write or call Clarence from Georgia to let him know of my arrival.

The sun slunk away toward the sea, drawing its pink and orange robes behind it. Cloud formations spiralled large and sinisterly colourful like an El Greco painting. By six o'clock, all the visible world would have fled into the darkness, but I would reach Clarence's house before then. The fifteen-minute drive took me across Bridge Road, up Station Hill past Glendairy prison, and past my old high school, Combermere, in Waterford. I passed the National Stadium, turned right up Green Hill and into the parish of St. Thomas where Clarence lived.

I remembered his coral stone house perched on a ridge that had a panoramic view of the luscious St. George valley in the southeast. I had last spoken to Clarence about a year and a half ago. I recalled how he had complained of still not getting any of his novels published after all these years. He had sounded bitter, resentful. He had been particularly disappointed about not getting the novel about George Washington published. He'd had high hopes for that one. There was a certain popular appeal to it, Washington's year of wild oats in Barbados. Of course, I had taken Clarence's word for this. I had no proof, and had sought none, of whether he had ever set foot on Barbadian soil. During our last conversation, Clarence had indicated that he was seriously considering emigrating to New York where his oldest son lived. 'To be near the publishing centres,' he said. But, having put in nearly thirty years in the Civil Service and not wanting to lose any retirement benefits, he had put that idea on hold. I got the impression that Clarence was venting his frustrations, but had no intention of leaving Barbados at all.

I swung off Jackson Main Road and slowly climbed Shop Hill. Not far ahead, on the right side of the road, I saw the little yellow Christian Mission which had always been my landmark to Clarence's house. But I couldn't recall if the church had been painted the same colour fifteen or so years ago. I turned into the cart road next to the church and descended a steep slope hedged with little wooden chattel houses. This small neighbourhood, modest in appearance, emitted a quiet pride in its neatly-trimmed hedges of crotons and hibiscus plants, the well-swept areas surrounding each house, and the glossy outer paint on the houses made brighter by the rays of the sun now sliding towards the sea. I climbed another steep hill which then gradually sloped downwards into Clarence's yard. The two-storey house, part coral stone, part cement brick, had been inherited from his father, a former police officer in the days when being a police officer in Barbados carried much prestige. Clarence's mother, now completely blind, lived in a separate building a few yards from him.

I parked next to a green Datsun, got out and walked down some red brick steps shaded by a large flamboyant, along a cement path that was hedged with luscious ginger lilies, crotons, and aloes, and came to a high, bolted wrought iron door at the front of the house. The wooden door behind the wrought iron one was open.

'Anybody home?' I shouted, holding on to the wrought iron bars with both hands and peering inside. A dog yapped in response. It continued yapping but never appeared. Then I heard someone call my name.

'Alphonso?' A man in white shorts and an unbuttoned short-sleeved plaid shirt appeared on the staircase which led into the living room. He approached me with a crawling gait buttoning his shirt as he came.

'Hey,' Clarence said. He appeared at once surprised and excited. He reached over to a mahogany side table and took up a key to open the padlock on the wrought iron door. 'Wha', I ain' even know you in de island. Come in, man.'

'The dog all right?'

155

'Yeah. He out back.' Clarence had the habit of punctuating his words with snorts as if he had some kind of respiratory ailment. That was another reason why I wasn't convinced he really intended to emigrate to New York with its harsh winters. I had detected this snorting some years ago during one of our telephone conversations.

'It's de cigarettes,' Clarence had told me. 'Burning out de frigging lungs, man.' When I asked him why he didn't quit, he said, 'Shoot, man. Yuh got to die from something.'

This time, I made no comment about his voice, but I was surprised and concerned by his appearance. For a man in his late fifties, he seemed much older. He had lost a lot of weight and seemed less energetic than I remembered him. It was true fifteen years had passed, but the physical change in him seemed frightfully exaggerated. His hair had turned completely grey, and about four or five deep furrows, etched permanently in his forehead, gave him a quizzical look.

He took me into his den and ushered me to sit on a brown couch. Before joining me, Clarence went to the far corner of the room and turned on the television set. I thought this rather odd, especially since he appeared to have done it self-consciously, with a certain hesitancy, as if unsure he was doing the right thing. It was almost as if he sought refuge in the television set, some sort of moral support. I wondered why. A soap opera was about to start. Clarence turned towards me, realized I was distracted, took a step backward, and lowered the volume on the set. He sat beside me on the couch, and I inquired about his health and about his mother. Everything was the same, he said. I told him why I had come to the island, or at least the surface reasons, and he appeared sympathetic regarding my story about the stolen furniture.

'Wha', how family life treating you?' he asked.

'Not too good right now. Simone and I are just about separated. What about you? You still married? I have to meet your wife.'

156

'Damn right, I am,' Clarence said with a resurrection of his old boisterousness. 'This man must have his door mat.' He grunted as he said this, his tone contemptuous.

'Well, where is she?'

'Well,' Clarence began, snorting, no longer able to conceal the truth, 'she's living in Pegwell with the other two children, man. I here on my own.' He spoke with his old libertine tone, which smouldered beneath the emaciated frame. But I sensed he was uncomfortable, and I didn't pursue the topic.

'You said she was a Black American?' Clarence asked.

'Who? My wife?'

Clarence nodded.

'Yes,' I said. 'Simone is a Black American.'

'Shite, man,' Clarence stamped his foot on the floor. 'I warned you 'bout those fockers, you know. You couldn' do any better than that, Alphonso?' Clarence averted his glance toward the TV. I stared at him, puzzled by the shifts in his tone. Was he joking or was he serious?

'What?' I asked.

'Black American women're the worst women in the Western world, man,' he said, his gaze still fixed on the set. 'I heard too many horror stories 'bout them. They're the worse. Ask one of those fockers to make you a cup of coffee, and they'll ask you why de fock you don't get it yourself.' Any possible ambiguity disappeared in his bluntness and intensity. He looked at me with a mischievous grin, like someone deliberately trying to unsettle another and taking a sadistic pleasure in doing so.

'Simone's a fine woman, man. I'm the reason why our relationship on the rocks, not her. How can you generalize like that? That's like saying all West Indian males are studs. You don't even know Simone.'

I began to associate Clarence's voice with that of the rude customs officer, with Verona, John, and all the negatives

157

that I'd encountered since my arrival on the island. It seemed as though while the island had progressed industrially, it had also developed a new code of rudeness. From Clarence, the only one of my old friends in Barbados with whom I had kept in touch, the insult hurt me deeply. It left me speechless. How was I to respond to such open and unprovoked ugliness? Should I just leave? Clarence hadn't even offered me a drink.

'So what else happening up in the States, Alphonso?' Clarence asked in an angry, brusque tone, his chin pushed high in the air, his Adam's apple rising and falling. What had I said or done to upset Clarence in this way? Immediately after I told him about my promotion at Wesslar, I regretted saying it, for his face became livid with denial and rage, as if my disclosure was somehow a deliberate attempt to belittle him, as if I were deliberately being boastful so as to make him feel bad.

'It must be awful working for those White people up there,' he said, snorting louder than before. 'They must be making your ass shite, man.'

'Nah, man,' I replied, no longer unsure of how I should respond. 'I don't have a chip on my shoulder (as one of my White friends keep telling me). So my life's no different than if I were here, really.' I, too, had gotten upset. I felt something retaliatory, something acidic gathering on my tongue.

'Actually,' I continued, about to spit the acid out, 'there's a big difference. I'm making a hell of a lot more money.' To try to liberate myself from the bad feelings welling up in me, I laughed loudly, expansively, as we used to do at The Pink Pelican restaurant. Clarence grinned in dry knots. Then the grin petered into a sneer.

'You fellas with two degrees are something else,' he said. 'You academics.'

'You call an engineer an academic?'

'Yes, a focking academic.'

'Are you saying graduate university education is unimportant?'

'Yeeeeeessss,' Clarence bellowed. He snorted more frequently now, and his eyes widened with rage. I'd had enough of his insults.

'What has happened to you, my friend? You've not only turned into a bigot and a misogynist, but an idiot as well,' I said. 'All you've done since I came here is put me down. It wasn't me who refused to publish your novels.'

My acidity seemed to have struck him hard. With raging feet, he leapt from the couch.

'Asshole!' he shouted and stamped the floor. Snorting, he turned and walked off toward the kitchen. As he passed the television set, he reached over and angrily turned the volume knob so high that the speakers rumbled and rattled. Clarence's back was a wall that I sensed would never come down for me. I watched him open the fridge door and take something out. Then he turned around with what looked like a beer in his hand. Without looking up, he said something which the competing voices from the television made indecipherable. Clarence then raised his head and shouted,

'I've had enough of you! Please leave!'

For a few seconds, I didn't move or reply. Then, Clarence, rooted to where he stood, slammed the refrigerator door and shouted, 'Go along, man! I said go along!'

It was over. Our friendship was over.

CHAPTER TWELVE

In spite of the hurt, I drove away from Clarence's house with the feeling that some process of resolution had begun, as if the open-ended parts of my life were, one by one, carefully being closed, carefully being concluded. Instead of sorrow and loss, I felt a curious relief as if some wind blew inside me that bore the promise of rest and peace. But this feeling was cautioned by the nudging of another element flowing beneath that hopeful wind, a strong sea current that prodded and tugged my past from side to side. How long could I put off the inevitable? Recoiling, I thrust my thoughts onto Lucinda, Denise, and yes... Simone. For the first time since I arrived, I had a desperate hunger to talk to them. It was more than hunger. It was necessity.

I swung the car off the road into the first shopping plaza I came to and called from a pay phone outside a grocery. Simone answered. I told her all that had happened since my arrival. Her voice sounded uncannily calm, but I forced myself not to comment on it. Under other circumstances I would have resented her tone, taking it for religious confidence and power and control.

'How're the girls?' I asked.

'They're all fine. Hold on. I'll get them for you. When you finish chatting with them, hold for me. There's a letter here from Wesslar that maybe you'd like me to open.'

Lucinda and Denise sounded a bit tired, sleepy, but they

pushed against the tiredness, glad to hear me. They had returned to school. They sounded happy. We reminisced about some of the games we used to play. Their favourite, 'The Little Mermaid', which we played in the community swimming pool. They, the mermaids; I, the rescuing prince.

'Sorry things didn't work out with your friend,' Simone said on her return.

'Nah. Just another example of what Barbados does to its artists, that's all. One more casualty. But things may change for the better. There's a new progressive party running in the upcoming elections. Maybe things may get better here if they win. Who knows?'

The calmness of my voice surprised me, but I was equally aware of the subterranean urges, like stirring anemones, from which I had yet to be released. I wanted to tell Simone about them. Concealing them for so long had become almost unbearable. Deciding to meet them and then recoiling at the last minute was exhausting me. I wanted rest. I wanted full release! But I caught myself in time. What would it help to overwhelm Simone now, separated as we were. My fears had been securely locked and bolted for most of my life. How could she even understand it all in just a few minutes of telephone conversation? I quickly pulled my past back from off my tongue before it took flight.

'That mail from Wesslar,' Simone said. 'Would you like me to open it?'

'Yes.'

Simone returned in a few seconds. I heard the tearing of the envelope and the opening of the correspondence inside. A lengthy silence followed.

'Which do you want to hear first? The good news or bad news?'

'Let's hear the bad news first,' I said with growing apprehension. The bad news was that some fifteen hundred Wesslar Aluminium employees, from clerks to engineers, were to be retrenched over the next few months. They would be given sixty-day severance packages. I started to feel listless and drily empty, like someone who'd received news of the sudden death of a relative. I knew the company had been engaged in nationwide downsizing, but I'd had no fears about my own security. Seniority, ten years of service, and their approval of my impending transfer, had not encouraged any thoughts of job loss. But had my requests for transfers been a determining factor in choosing me for retrenchment, even though the current transfer had already been granted? Had Wesslar had a change of heart in the light of my perceived instability? Then Simone said, 'The good news is that all Senior Supervisors will receive a 10 percent pay cut. You still got your job.'

'Thank God!' I exclaimed. 'I should've asked for the good news first. You really had me scared there for a while.' When Simone asked me when I was returning, I fell silent for a moment and then told her I planned to extend my stay in Barbados for another few weeks to visit my parent's graves and to observe the upcoming elections.

I hung up the phone, feeling drained, like a man who, knocked down by powerful waves, manages to get to his feet and feels the wind blow on his face with a promise of rest. What would I have done if I'd lost my job? The children's educational fund? Simone not yet secure in a job? How would they have survived? I would probably have tried private consultancy in Atlanta, which was just two hours from Augusta. I would still have been near my daughters. With thankful thoughts over still having my job, I went to bed.

I awoke next morning with the sense of anticipation over Christopher's meeting. When I arrived at his office just after nine o'clock, it had already started. There were five people around Christopher's desk and he introduced me as his old high school mate.

'I'm trying to get him to stay in the island,' he said. 'This man has one of the best brains around. We should benefit from it and not the U.S.'

The others laughed. Clockwise, I shook the hands of Phillip Jordan, Phyllis Scantlebury, Julian Gittens, Judy Brathwaite – who was wearing a loose cotton dress that resembled (or was) a maternity dress – and, finally, giving me an expansive grin that revealed dark-coloured gums, and little laugh lines at the outer edges of his eyes, Ryan Proute.

Christopher had spoken so highly of him that I felt genuinely honoured to meet him.

'Good luck in the upcoming elections,' I said.

They were looking at some stapled handouts that showed a breakdown of the shareholding assets of the Mutual Life Assurance Society in most of the island's major companies, in firms that manufactured rum and fine liqueurs, shipping and trading companies, grocery chains, insurance companies, manufacturers of household paints, real estate, computer software and office equipment, confectionery products, photo centres, department store chains, the Barbados Telephone Company, Barbados External Telecommunications Ltd., and Barbados Light and Power Co.

What these statistics showed was the racial concentration of economic power. The companies were all run by Whites. The fact of race itself would not have been a problem had that elite group been interested in sharing power, but they were not.

'As you can see,' Philip turned to me, 'we still under economic apartheid.'

Phyllis said, 'Barrow felt if Blacks got university education, then the Whites would feel confident to power-share with us, let us be part of the financial decision-making in their companies. But he was dead wrong. Except for a token here and there, they have no interest whatsoever in letting us in.' Phyllis wore a small mini-Afro hairstyle, small black-rimmed eyeglasses, light make-up. She looked well-toned, the kind of woman who worked out at least twice a week.

'We know the problem, and we know the solution,' Christopher said.

'Of course,' Ryan Proute added. 'When we win the elections it will be essential to refashion private sector control, not along racial lines but along the lines of social justice.'

I was taken with his confidence. 'When we win the elections,' he had said. Not 'If we win.' I could see how he could have been regarded as arrogant. His opponents had said as much in their campaigning, but I saw that his aura was really an assuredness, a deep-seated self-confidence, the kind that always infuriated a person's enemies, who understood and feared such serious competition.

The following week, I accompanied Christopher to a BWP meeting in Trafalgar Square. Portable security fences had been strategically placed to reroute the city traffic. The press polls had indicated the BWP was ahead in popular support in the three-party race. Ryan Proute had made his ticket clear: the need for a political system that allowed economic justice for all. The White minority and Black middle class were his chief critics, but his popular appeal (especially amongst the youth and the underprivileged) explained why there was this sea of expectancy at Trafalgar Square.

He strode to the podium, and the swell of cheering from the crowd made it impossible for him to speak. He waited a few minutes, and then raised a hand.

'Thank you... thank you, Brothers and Sisters. Three weeks from today, on the eve of our thirtieth year of Independence, we'll be able to truly claim the beginnings of real independence when we have Economic Justice For All!' The audience roared in support of the BWP's now famous slogan.

'This foolishness can't continue.' Ryan raised his right hand again to silence the crowd. 'Doesn't Barbados pride itself on having one of the oldest democracies in this hemisphere? Democracy for who? Not for me, Brothers and Sisters, and not for you. We have come here this evening to say we are tired. We are tired of the show, tired of being seen as the rulers of this country when we really aren't. We want real rulership. We deserve it. Our children deserve it. And we all know that real rulership comes through economic power, not political power. We have delivered our manifesto to you... Barbadians. Not Black Barbadians, not White Barbadians, but all Barbadians who are interested in fairness and the rights of others. And we promise you, when we become the new government, not to spare any effort in addressing this economic imbalance in our country. Our existing legislation pertaining to the private sector will be changed to assure a place in this island for our children, their children, and their children's children.'

Ryan spoke for over an hour. His voice never faltered. Trafalgar Square was thick with his energy and his vision. It filled the courtyard of the Parliament buildings and eddied down Broad Street. The day after the Trafalgar Square meeting, newspapers were full of warring sentiments for and against Ryan. One, in particular, caught my attention. Its headline read: **MUTUAL BOARD HEAD SPEAKS OUT**.

The article carried a photo of a bespectacled Geoffrey Simpson gesticulating in his office for the camera. In the article, Geoffrey called Ryan a communist and a racist. He said that Ryan's economic reform measures violated the Constitution because they were racially motivated.

'If the BWP is elected, Barbados is doomed,' Geoffrey said. 'Our economy will be crippled. The tourists will flee.'

I was so incensed by this statement that the same afternoon I went to Simpson's Enterprises in Bridgetown with the intention of letting him know what I thought of his remarks.

As I headed for his office on the top floor of his Broad Street complex, I started remembering how Geoffrey's father had helped mine so many years ago and that thought began to soften my approach. Out of loyalty to both our fathers, as Simpson's son, he at least deserved my verbal courtesy instead of my anger. I inched my way towards the secretary's desk and introduced myself. She buzzed Geoffrey, told him who I was, and ushered me into the office. As I entered, Geoffrey broke off a low conversation he was having with an elderly man seated next to him and looked up at me.

'Well, hello... Hutsy's boy,' he said, torturing his face into a smile which was soon aborted. There was none of the bouncy cordiality he'd exhibited on the plane. I thought perhaps he felt I'd come to ask him for a favour and had assumed a more formal manner to deal with it. He flushed deeply, seized, it seemed, by a sudden and embarrassing inability to find anything more to say. My right hand went out towards him. He hesitated briefly, as if surprised by the gesture, and then reached out his hand. I, too, could find nothing to say right then, but I nodded, shook his hand, and took a seat. Our families had been connected deeply, intimately, even if within a framework of masters, mis-tresses and household servants. Despite that context, all that time and familiarity must have touched Geoffrey emotionally. He had practically been raised by my mother. Until now, I had felt much more removed from such notions of intimacy, but the obligatory need to be courteous to him told me that I, too, in some strange way, had been touched. I, too, had been shadowed by such bonds and had been influenced by them, if indirectly, through all those stories my parents brought home of their interactions with the Simpsons. Good stories. Bad stories. And they had lodged themselves in my memory without my conscious consent, had remained buried there all these years, had risen now, when I'd least expected them, resurrected by this contact. We were another generation, but perhaps it was still only in education that we stood on level ground. My discomfort was rising. We looked at each other, trustfully, mistrustfully, separated by a wooden table and a racial divide to which we both were inexorably linked.

Finally Geoffrey said, 'I'm surprised to see you here. What can I do for you?'

'I read yesterday's newspaper,' I said. 'Your remarks surprised me. I thought things would be different in Barbados by now.'

'And I thought you'd be getting some sea baths after being away for so long,' Geoffrey said. Turning to the man next to him, he added, 'His father worked for us years ago.' *Worked for us.* There was an ironic distancing in his tone, as if he might have misread me on the plane and now felt the need for immediate reassessment. It was that new view, one which perhaps saw the necessity of taking sides, that would have made him assume the hierarchical and historical stance of employer, of owner. I wasn't surprised when he suddenly picked up the phone and said, 'You'll have to excuse me. I have a very important call to make and I'm running late for a meeting.' He held the receiver to his chest with both hands, reclined in his brown swivel chair, and waited for me to leave.

I said, 'You're going to lose, you know that. It's a new day for us.'

Geoffrey's face turned beet-red, and he started to rise from the chair. The elderly man next to him put a hand on his shoulder and steered him back down into his seat.

On election night, at Christopher's invitation, I headed to the BWP's headquarters on Roebuck Street. It had rained all evening, not a heavy downpour, but a light, steady, cleansing rain. The car park glistened with hundreds of wet vehicles. People, umbrellas raised, were negotiating the puddles that had collected there: some men hopped over them while women held up their skirts or rolled their pants up a few inches higher.

Inside the building, three television monitors relayed results from the polling stations. The Democratic Labour Party was showing worst. The race was being fought between the Barbados Labour Party and the BWP. Slowly and steadily the BWP gained and held the lead. The charged atmosphere gradually turned festive and the temperature rose as the crowd of party members increased. Ryan watched the polling results with a confident gleam. Occasionally I heard him laugh his expansive laugh; on other occasions, he sat, his chin on interwoven hands, staring intently at the monitor. With the announcement of the final results around midnight, tuk calypso music steadily gyrated through the room, and people danced, drank beers, cheered and shouted for victory. Four men hoisted Ryan in the air while others toasted him. I found Christopher grinning like a school boy. He hugged me and gave me his beer. As if by magic, another beer appeared in his hand. Phyllis was with him. She seemed even more beautiful tonight. She glistened, the caramel skin, the little Afro, the well-textured lips, the bottom one protruding slightly further than the top. She wore a black and green striped cotton dress reaching just above her knees. Our eyes met, and suddenly it was as if only the two of us existed in that room. I reeled under the blow of attraction. I wasn't sure I was ready for this. But before I could rationalize myself into recovery, Phyllis reached out her arms to me.

'Come on, Alphonso. Let's dance,' she said, beginning to uncoil to the music. I looked at Christopher who smiled a 'Go on' smile. I looked at Phyllis again.

'Don't tell me you've forgotten how to dance to calypso.' Oh how she beamed.

'Oh no,' I said, slowly uncoiling towards her. 'I could never forget that.' We danced and laughed. Until then, in spite of my interest, excitement, and increasing sense of pride, I had still been a passive observer. My hesitancy about dancing with Phyllis was a symptom. As we danced, I knew although I still remained an observer, I had now become a more active one. She had chosen me, and this assumed for me a meaning beyond mere male-female attraction. It signified for me a social homecoming, a re-emersion into the river of the tribe.

Julian, Judy and Phillip joined us, brimming with merriment and triumph. The press suddenly appeared everywhere. Ryan, flanked by other prospective members of his cabinet and the executive of the Alliance for Economic Democracy, settled in a chair for questions from a TV reporter who, effectively, was now in Ryan's employ.

The reporter asked, 'Your intention to take power from the mercantile elite, to stimulate a more widespread and equitable control over the means of production... Do you anticipate goodwill from other parliamentarians who are not members of the BWP?'

'I sincerely hope so. It's the only way forward for our country. I hope the corporate elite to which you refer will finally do the right thing and realize that for our country to face the challenges of the future, the ethnic majority must be an essential part of our economic policies.'

'I know you haven't been sworn in yet, but, Prime Minister Proute, what are you looking forward to most now after your victory tonight?'

'My wife, Waveney. I look forward to hugging my wife, my son and two daughters, and getting a full night's rest.'

Phyllis and I were still together when most of the party members and supporters had left.

'You must be really exhausted from all the activity,' I said.

'Man, you kidding? That's an understatement. But, you know, none of us ain' sleeping tonight. Too much adrenaline, man. We heading over to my place. You coming?'

'Sure,' I said.

I had felt their fear, their hope, their commitment, and I had witnessed the realization of their goal. *Was there any better way to live than in service to one's people?*

Hundreds of White Barbadians with dual citizenship were the first to flee. They cashed in as many of their assets as they could and left to join family in England, Canada, the U.S., New Zealand, Australia. Those who couldn't leave or wouldn't leave because they had too much to lose, threatened to boycott the country, to pull every advertisement from the Government-owned Caribbean Broadcasting Corporation, to layoff thousands of workers in the private sector, to shut down their hotels and cripple tourism. The Barbadian economy would come to a halt. With the support of the Black middle class, the corporate minority's blackmail forced the BWP to make a placatory statement about its plans. I sensed that Ryan cared too much for the country to risk the economic and social chaos that would ensue should the corporate elite carry out its threats.

But Ryan had an alternative plan which he divulged in an exclusive interview in the leading Saturday newspaper. His radical changes were announced to tie in with the party's Saturday victory parade. Ryan and his government would nationalize all the foreign-owned banks. He would replace these with branches of the existing government-owned Bank of Barbados. While it was true the corporate elite had its own capital and did not rely on the government for loans, this initiative was designed to give Black businesses the kind of loan support needed to expand, hire more staff, and offer real competition to the White-owned sector. If the Black businesses gained the support of most of the population, in time, the profits of the minority businesses would shrink and the country would be less vulnerable to White economic blackmail. He feared that the greatest obstacle to this policy wouldn't be the Whites but the Black middle-class who

170

might remain loyal to the corporate elite and their retail enterprises. After all, many of them were employed by that sector.

'The Black middle class,' Ryan was quoted as saying in the interview, 'if they could only see beyond the brevity of their own lives and support us, real economic power for their children would be guaranteed. The Black middle class. They're the last stronghold of White supremacy.'

His words resonated in me. All my life I had deeply desired to be a member of that class. I had hoped for it; I had longed for it. This had been my primary motivation for leaving Barbados; to be successful, to escape the wrenching poverty. I had achieved that and for the past ten years had lived a middle-class life in the US. Now, to hear Ryan speak of the Bajan middle class as the guarantors of an unjust Barbadian society, was to see myself objectively, as it were, for the first time. I had never looked at my actions as having any implications beyond their effect on my immediate family. The Black middle class in Barbados included people like me who had been raised here and received higher education abroad. Unlike me, they had returned home on completion of their studies to establish themselves, to escape the pressures of living overseas with all the racial anxiety that sapped one's energies. But return for them, men and women in their twenties or thirties, had become a sort of retirement, a retirement not from eight-to-four work, but from struggle. They had become satisfied. To own a six-figure brick house, a fashionable car, a satellite dish, and shop in Miami or New York City during their annual vacations, was all they wanted. No more struggle. They had achieved their personal goals and had become completely detached from the lives of the rest of the population, including, I saw now, their own children. For present gratification and prosperity based on income, they had forfeited their offspring's economic future because the country's wealth, and hence the country's future, was not in their hands, but in the hands of those for whom they worked.

I had caught a glimmer of a potentially new Barbados, and in the light of what was happening to my marriage back in the US, it wasn't surprising that I began courting the idea of finding a place in this new Barbados. I had left the island, because I could see no meaningful opportunities. If the BWP realized its goals, would there be a place for me in Barbados at last? But what about my children in the US? I would miss them horribly.

Now, as the victory parade began, the black convertible sedan, hood drawn back, passed a fence pulsing with a reddish-pink profusion of flowering vines and slid out on to the main road. I followed. I could see Julian Gittens and a BWP candidate named Ronald Welch in the back seat of the convertible. Ryan Proute sat in the front passenger seat, waving to the public. Christopher drove the sedan with a slow measured moving of his head from side to side, acknowledging the world yet no doubt concentrating on the driving. Behind me was a large truck packed with jubilant party members. Through my rear-view mirror, I recognized Phyllis and a more visibly pregnant Judy Brathwaite. Phillip Jordan was there, too, bowed legs writhing underneath him to the calypso music which blared from two giant speakers mounted on top of the truck. Several other cars of supporters followed. The motorcade drove past the Queen Elizabeth Hospital and down River Road. As we approached the Fairchild Street Bus Terminal, I saw the teeming Saturday shoppers moving in and out of the terminal. All along the route into the city (the constituency which Ryan had won), the motorcade had been cheered by passers-by and horn-tooting motorists. These affirmations continued as we circled Independence Square and drove slowly across the Chamberlain Bridge. We passed the Wharf,

Cavans Lane and then began the slower drive up Broad Street, the city's main street. The pulsating sounds from the Party's float cast a spirit of festivity along the route. Press photographers flanked the sides of the street, cameras raised, needing no flashes in the bright mid-morning light.

Then there was a fracturing noise, like a loud fire cracker. I looked ahead at the others to see their reaction. I wasn't sure if it was some kind of firework, a backfiring vehicle, but when I saw Julian Gittens slump on Ronald Welch with blood running down the side of his face, I knew what had happened.

Those on the float started shouting, 'Get down! Somebody shooting!' The convertible swiftly halted, and I saw a hand reach forward and push Ryan to the floor. I recalled Christopher's account of Harcourt Hilary's death-threats eight years earlier. In that moment of recollection, another shot sounded, and I felt a searing pain in my left shoulder. The left side of my body felt as if it was on fire. A numbness began to spread over me, and everything, the voices of the screaming crowd, the glimpses of fleeing people, the calypso music rumbling in the giant speakers, became vague and distant.

CHAPTER THIRTEEN

I'd received no more than a deep flesh wound. Julian wasn't as lucky. He died from the gunshot wound to his head. Julian's death and the attempted assassination of Ryan Proute shook us all and showed us the lengths to which those opposed to the new government would go. Who ordered the shooting? Although the gunman was never caught, we felt certain that someone from the elite corporate sector had been behind it. I remained hospitalized for a week. On my release, I took it slowly, slept a lot. As my strength returned, I did some light work around the house. Phyllis had visited me every day in the hospital. Now she came over 'to help out', she said. She could do nothing for my physical convalescence, but her affection touched my emotions in the most wondrous way.

I had been transported, through Christopher and his movement, to the heights of a vision of possibility for my country, though it was now tinged with the sadness of Julian's death. For the first time in my life I understood what it meant to be a part of a cause, something larger than myself, something that would endure and touch the lives of people I would never even meet or get to know. Now there were everyday realities creeping back into my consciousness, tempering my romantic inclinations. I had been able to get the prospective tenants to hold off occupancy of my parents' house until after elections. But I knew I couldn't keep delaying them indefinitely without risking losing their business. I knew I had to make a decision within the next week or two. All the obstacles I'd experienced since my arrival on the island (rude officials, thieving relatives, a broken friendship) were, I knew, nothing to compare with what lay ahead and what I had put off until the very last. I had to admit to myself that I'd been perversely glad to have had these obstacles to overcome, that along with my eagerness to become involved with Christopher and the BWP they'd provided a welcome distraction. But they had brought me only a partial covering of rest. The truth was that, in an unconscious sense, each day had grown more laden with challenge. Here I was, in Barbados, repeating the pattern of running and hiding in constant activity, just as I had done in the USA. But it wasn't working. A protean fear, present yet suppressed due to all the frantic activity of the past weeks, had built forcefully, relentlessly, taking clearer shape all the time. And now, with other competitors out of the way, it formed tangibly inside me, filling me, forking, proliferating, pushing its way through my pores, penis, alimentary tract, indeed, every space it could find. I ached at every point. Next morning, around nine o'clock, I headed for Westbury Cemetery.

A yellow wall surrounded the island's only public burial ground. Above the wall, several royal palms stretched like ostriches. A portion of the wall, broken near the gate through which I'd entered and just inches from the roadside, looked as if it would collapse. A stream of bilge-like water coursed through the gutter between the road and the wall. The cemetery was a huge lake of headstones, most of them simply inscribed slabs, a few towering columnar edifices with Romanesque arches, all coming alive in the growing light.

I drove up to the main office, a small brick building to which a little grey church was attached. The belfry's steeple, like a giant needle, pricked the seamless morning sky. At its base, a faded pink shingled roof capped a windowed section. At the base of this section, another wider roof spread out its newer pink shingles like a fan over another section that also contained a window. At the very bottom of the bell tower was a closed, high-arched, wooden door. The tower ascended like a hope against the faded grey walls of the church building. I entered the office and presented my parents' death certificates to an elderly man with grey hair at the sides of his otherwise bald head and asked for directions to the graves. The elderly cemetery clerk told me in a raspy voice that I was in luck. The wooden cross which Aunt Lolita had insisted on acquiring had not yet been removed from Elroy's spot in the normally unmarked section. Elroy could not be buried with my parents since my parents' grave lot (which had been donated by the Simpsons) was still too fresh at the time of his death, and there were no other lots for purchase.

I left the car next to the church building and walked, with growing unease, in the direction the old man had indicated. I nodded to male and female cemetery weeders as I passed the grave sites. Some of them worked, while others squatted under mahogany trees, or leaned against their rakes and hoes. Most nodded back at me. Clusters of dried-up flowers mottled several of the graves and one or two bore freshly-made wreaths of crimson orchids, the blood-red spherical heads of ixora, heliconias with their bright red and yellow alternating bracts, and ginger lilies.

At last I arrived at the spot where my parents' grave was supposed to be. My eyes scoured the area, seeing and not seeing. I inched through the grass surrounding the graves, conscious of a lump gathering in my throat. It lodged there and then spread outward like almond tree branches through my limbs. *The middle of the three graves*, the clerk had said.

176

Swaying with vertigo, I hovered by the outer grave on the right, not wanting to continue any further. I managed to move to the foot of the grave, but, once there, I wanted to run away as fast and as far as I could. I tried to move, but my feet had become glued to the spot. As much as I strained to look away, I could not. An invisible hand had seized me. Living ghost hand. I broke into a sweat, and I felt cold streams run down my body and my legs.

I felt my body still straining to move, to turn away, to escape. As I stood there I felt fibrous tissue pressing against the Reeboks and then bursting through them and, as I looked down, I marvelled that I could see through the grass and the soil at my feet, could see the ancestral roots issuing out from my feet, growing longer and longer as they penetrated the soil in both directions and encircled the grave. I wept now, uncontrollably. My knees buckled and, assuming a squatting position, I placed my right hand on top of the cold slab. How long I remained there with my hand on the slab, I couldn't say, but I wept until the lump in my throat had fully dissolved. Looking to my left, I saw a stray root needling towards the poor man's section, but after journeying a few feet, it suddenly stopped.

I moved in the direction of the aborted root hair. I stood at the quivering point where it ended and looked over the sea of headstones glistening in the now hard morning light. Eyes of the dead. Penetrating eyes of the past. I had to walk through them all, possessing and being possessed. After over fifteen years of procrastination, I arrived at the poor man's section, a wide basin of mould and overgrown nut grass, locally called 'the bone hole.' After a few years, with the flesh of the dead dissolved into dust, another body would be laid here, eternal strangers possessed by one another, possessing one another. I walked on, my eyes scouring the site. After some minutes I saw, sprouting from the right corner of the plot, a leaning, black wooden cross almost overgrown by muscular nut grass. Dew and rain had caused the rust from the nails to drip and etch itself like blood into the wood. I approached the grave and was barely able to read parts of the once white inscription: **-n Memory of El— Trevo- Hut— 1951-1985.** Aunt Lolita must have replaced the worn wooden cross occasionally over the years, and this one would have been the last to have been erected. As I made another step toward the cross, my right foot suddenly dropped into a hole at least eight inches deep. Was it Elroy pulling me into his rest? His weariness? Terrified, I reached down and drew back the grass from around my foot. The grave site had sunk about twelve inches over the area where the last coffin, now no doubt completely disintegrated, had been laid. I passed a hand slowly over my sweating head and looked up into a nearby sandbox tree. I couldn't see the birds in it, but I could hear a choir of wood doves and crows warbling dirges from the high branches.

Composing myself as best as I could, I braced for some other strong emotion to overcome me, but I felt nothing. I stared at the rotting cross leaning at an angle of almost forty-five degrees, stared at the basin of earth choked with grass. I heard the warbling birds, felt my back beginning to melt under the blasts of the sun. Everything was so concrete, so ordinary. All I had felt was an entirely predictable alarm when my foot had stumbled down an unseen hole. Were all my thoughts of Elroy an elaborate build-up to something as meaningless as a hole in the ground? Had my fears existed merely because I had allowed a space for them? Had the secrecy surrounding Elroy created a soil of mystery in which the weeds of fear had blossomed, weeds of self-pity and self-punishment? But where was Elroy in all this, the smiling child in the wheelchair I had never seen, the brother I had never acknowledged as mine. Elroy in death was no different from anyone else in death. It was the living Elroy I needed to embrace. An idea struck me.

CHAPTER FOURTEEN

I turned left on Black Rock Main Road and, minutes later, pulled into Gracewood Home for the Mentally and Physically Handicapped. It took an hour or so for the clerks in Records to find out who had been Elroy's doctor. He finally came into the lobby, a short stocky man with a bald spot in the centre of his head. I sensed it was him and, before the receptionist could say anything, I had risen from the chair where I sat. We shook hands vigorously, though for me it was all nervous energy. Dr. Bane invited me to accompany him to his office some yards down the main corridor.

'Cerebral palsy,' he said, as he closed the door behind him and ushered me to a green leatherette couch. 'A particularly severe case.' He spoke almost as if he were addressing himself. He coupled this delicacy of speech with an uncanny precision of words and a careful and caring remembrance of details of the case through Elroy's name alone. 'He was with us for a very long time. We got to care about him very deeply.'

'How did he get like this?' I asked.

'A delayed caesarian delivery preventing the flow of oxygen to the brain. As a little boy, there were flickers of hope, but as the years went on that changed. It was painful for me, personally, to watch him get worse and worse. I was with him from the start.' An aching line seemed to appear on the doctor's smooth face. He plucked a handkerchief from a pocket of his white shirt jack and softly mopped his brow. He seemed genuinely pained, but the ease with which he spoke and acted indicated that he had made many such speeches during his career. He had been standing next to his desk all the while, and now he went and sat behind the desk.

'Did he ever talk? Did he ever say anything?'

'Oh, when he was a boy, he'd try to make words, that sort of thing. He had a lovely smile, when he did smile. All the nurses loved his smile. But, you know,' the doctor sighed heavily, 'after a while, I think he gave up. The medication had side effects. Seizures. As time went on, they grew worse. He fractured his vertebrae. There was also the swelling of the gums. Very painful. But he was a brave child. Elroy was a strong child. Most of us felt his passing was merciful.'

'Yes, perhaps it was,' I said with tears in my eyes. The information which the doctor gave me turned like a knife in my bowels. But I was also experiencing a sense of relief as Elroy's illness was finally being demystified. 'Well, I'm glad I came to see you, Doctor. You have no idea how much talking to you has helped.'

Doctor Bane stood up and walked to the front of the desk. He folded his arms and leaned on the edge of the desk.

'I take it your parents never told you about Elroy's condition. I know of their tragic deaths. But don't hold it against them. Remember, this is Barbados. And years ago, there was much less tolerance towards such disability. Don't blame them. They were probably afraid of making you afraid.'

The doctor unfolded his arms and approached me. He placed a hand on my shoulder. I nodded. Then I stood up and shook his hand.

'Thank you, Doctor Bane. You've been very helpful.' Gaining specific information about Elroy's condition had not only given me some control over the fraternal ghost, it had given me a glimpse of Elroy himself. I knew my parents had tried to protect me by concealing Elroy. Knowing now what Elroy had suffered from, I was able to change the grotesque and anomalous image of a fat-cheeked baby with a man's body collapsed in a wheelchair to the more familiar image of a sufferer from cerebral palsy, an image which I had seen countless times on television programs. Now I could identify Elroy with the real world around me instead of with the unreal gothic nightmares my mind had constructed. This new perception took away the mystery, the secrecy, the misdirected flight of the imagination.

That afternoon, around three o'clock, I went into the old workshop in the yard and took out the rusty machete. I started at the front of the house where I began chopping down the grass and overgrown shrubs. I soon settled into an even chopping rhythm. The crisp cloudless sky was a blue throne for the sun, but a steady strong breeze made the heat bearable. My invasion into the miniature wood at the front of the house awakened a multitude of creatures. I chopped whole armies of millipedes into segments. Gathering some chopped grass into a pile, the slime from anguished slugs oozed over my hands and I dropped the grass instantly. I had always detested those hideous things. In Grazettes, there had been many of them. I remember my father rounding them up in the middle of the yard with a thin flat piece of wood, covering them with kerosene-soaked paper, and then setting the paper on fire. Parched and curled like oversized commas, the slugs would then be swept into an old grocery bag and thrown into the trash. With the blade of the machete, I turned over the bundle of grass I had dropped and, one by one, flicked the oozing things over the hedge and into the road. I imagined them roasting on the hot tar and curling into commas.

A group of brown butterflies, wings mottled with black dots, danced in the air above the Pride of Barbados hedge with its fernlike leaves and clusters of red blooms. Other smaller white butterflies glided over the oleander hedge and across the lawn. The fronds of the twin royal palms rattled like maracas in the steady breeze. I worked for a couple of hours and then sat on the front step to catch my breath. I leaned the machete against the step and scratched my itching arms which were covered with little bits of grass. I longed for a bath, but felt a responsibility to make the house as presentable as possible for the new tenants.

From where I sat, I could see a group of boys playing cricket not far down the road. For stumps, they used a rectangular piece of wood which they'd no doubt propped from behind with a stick. The bowler and fielder on the leg side had their backs to me, but I could see the faces of the batsman and the mid-off fielder. The latter stood on the vacant lot. The lads appeared to be between ten and fifteen years old. I heard their shouts, laughter, and occasional disagreeing tones. The bowler, left-handed and imitating the slow hunched crawl of Sir Gary Sobers, delivered and struck the stumps. The batsman shouted, 'Man, no, man! I didn' ready, man! I ain' out!' The others quickly gathered around him, and one of them attempted to wrench the bat from his hands. The batsman was adamant. He also looked like the oldest in the group. Soon, the others succumbed to his terrible mood and, frowning with defeat, resumed the game. The next ball was a full toss which the batsman struck high and hard. The furless tennis ball struck one of the royal palms, rolled along the grass and stopped a few feet from the step on which I sat. Smiling, I moved towards the ball. The young bowler came running up to the hedge.

'You guys having a good game? 'I asked. The boy nodded. 'But don't hit the ball too hard, you know. You don't want your parents to have to pay for broken windows.' I held the ball as I spoke.

The boy, hands held out in anticipation of my throw, said, 'You see how we out him just now and he say he wusn't out?'

I smiled. The boy, who looked about ten, folded his arms after I didn't throw the ball. Still slightly winded, baby-faced, barefooted, he wore khaki short pants and a white vest.

'What's your name, youngster?'

'Elroy.' I visibly started, and the ball dropped from my hand.

'Who you belong to?' I asked, picking up the ball again.

'Miss Lashley is my grandmother.'

'You're Miss Lashley's grandson?' The boy nodded. 'I didn't know Miss Lashley had grandchildren.'

'I got two sisters and a brother.' The lad was getting restless. He shuffled his feet and stuck his hands into his pants pockets. I stared at him, stared at the baby-fat cheeks glistening in health. Elroy was all right. Elroy was all right. I tossed the ball to the youngster.

'Throw it back to me,' I said. The baffled boy obeyed, and we stood there throwing the ball backwards and forwards, playing ball like brothers on the unevenly-cut grass. I laughed and laughed.

'You can't throw any harder than that?' I asked. Elroy bit into his lips and threw the ball with every bit of strength he could muster. The ball struck me on the right thigh and deflected to the left side of the house. Exaggerating the pain, I hopped after it. This amused Elroy, now apparently at ease, and he was still laughing when, throwing the ball in the air and re-catching it, I reappeared.

'Well, I'm convinced,' I said, laughing and feigning to throw the ball. When I finally did throw the ball, Elroy caught it and sped down the road to bowl again.

CHAPTER FIFTEEN

I continued to watch the boys play for a while longer until my sweat dried. A cumulus cloud partially covered the sun which had tilted sharply toward the sea. A bus roared from the nearby main road. I went into the yard and leaned the machete against the side of the back step. I itched all over, and my body yearned for a bath. I couldn't have one here, because the house had a shower but no tub. 'The sea!' I suddenly said aloud and with incomprehensible excitement, like an amnesiac suddenly recalling who he is. I hadn't been to the sea since my arrival. I went inside and gathered my swim suit, towel, and wallet. I removed my tennis shoes and jeans, stepped into the grey nylon Surf trunks, and then put on the jeans and shoes again. With the voices of the sea humming inside me, I headed for Gravesend Beach.

Twenty minutes later, I pulled into the parking lot of the Pebbles restaurant and parked next to an orange-coloured lifeguard tower. I got out and looked across at the open-sided restaurant where the heads of tourists concentrated over cocktails. On the outside of the restaurant, a large sign with a blue dolphin fish painted at the top gave the opening hours and some of the local dishes which it served. Dinner began at six o'clock and diners would, no doubt, be able to watch the sunset as they ate. The dishes included flying fish sandwiches, flying fish with rice and peas, and pudding and souse. I fondly remembered the latter and my mother's ritual preparation of it, how she stuffed the pig's intestines with grated sweet potato and a variety of chopped peppers and seasonings. The open end of the sausage would be tied with a piece of string and the sausage boiled. I recalled my mother instructing me not to talk too loudly or slam any doors, because the noise would cause the sausages to burst. It was a solemn thing, this making of black pudding. The souse comprised the pickled ear and other diced pieces of pork. These were steeped in a briny liquid which contained chopped red peppers, grated cucumber, and lime juice. Thinking about this dish made my mouth water and, after my sea bath, I decided I'd have it for dinner, washed down with a glass of lemonade.

I watched two women walk languidly across the car park in the direction of an hotel about a quarter mile or so up the road. One wore pink shorts, the other white. They held their straw hats to their heads, against the wind. Their loose unbuttoned cotton shirts swirled around and glimpses of bikini tops betrayed a recent engagement with the sea. I reached the rim of the beach and went down the wooden steps which ended on the sand. I slipped off my tennis shoes and the warm grains of sand foamed between and around my toes. I stepped over a star fish that had been washed up on the shore. Two small hermit crabs scuttled across my path and into the safety of their holes. A jogger in red swimming trunks with bulging chest muscles and biceps passed by, his eyes fastened on the area of sand directly before him. Not once did I see him look up. His black body shone with perspiration. Not long afterwards, a man and a woman jogged by, more casually. They talked and laughed like middle-aged lovers or a married couple still in love.

I laid the striped towel on the sand and placed my tennis shoes next to it, pulled the T-shirt over my head and stepped out of my jeans. I passed my thumbs around the inside of the trunks' elasticated waistline, stretched it and looked out to sea. High tide. The water calm, flat, perfectly aquamarine. Two parakeets and a white egret sped up and down over the water in a curious chasing game. I arrived at the water's edge and began to slowly walk along it. The cool water broke softly, churning sand and little pebbles and shells around my feet. My spirit rose, startled again by the beauty of the warm light and the colours. I had forgotten how overwhelming this Barbados seascape could be. It astonished me in the way that all natural wonders astonish: it humbled and made me aware I was part of a much larger reality. And, like a restored amnesiac, I recalled how each weekend and almost every day during the summer holidays, we neighbourhood boys would find our way to the nearest beach for swimming, diving, beach cricket. But from the age of fourteen or so, I had lost interest in the sea and had taken it for granted. Now I warmed to this reawakening of who I was and the salt-laden hand that had shaped my existence. Feeling loved, I reached out and took the hand.

My body hummed with liquid melodies. The sun rapidly descended to the horizon, igniting it and the lower sky in a carnival of red, crimson, and golden orange. I went fully under the water and rubbed my arms, chest, and legs with sand which I scooped up from the sea bed. I surfaced for air and went down again. For reasons which I cannot explain, I repeated this ritual three times. Then I floated on my back, looking up into the face of the light pink sky. I heard the water lapping and whispering its harmonies around my ears.

The black pudding and souse was as delicious as I had anticipated. I left the Pebbles around seven o'clock and came out to Bay Street. Instead of turning right in the direction from which I had come, I made a left turn towards the Esplanade. Just yards after I turned left on Bay Street, I saw a plaza on the left side of the road. It hadn't been there fifteen years ago. I did, however, recall coming here to a night club called Pandora's Hideaway. The club was situated on the top floor of a two-storey building. I pulled into the plaza, got out of the car, and followed an outer wrought-iron staircase to the second floor. What had formerly been Pandora's Hideaway was now a fitness centre. I went inside and a beaming young woman greeted me at the desk. She told me the centre was operated by her uncle, Earl Maynard, a former champion Barbados body builder who had won many major international titles before moving to California and getting into films. Now he had returned home and was running his own fitness centre. As I hadn't worked out since my arrival on the island, I signed up for a few sessions.

During the days that followed, I kept a steady routine of yard work in the mornings, work-out, lunch (which comprised the fitness centre's special food drink – made by Earl Maynard himself: a blend of egg protein, wheat germ, guavas, milk, and bananas), and an afternoon angelus of sea bathing. I broke this routine a couple of times to have lunch with Christopher. He and several executives of the Alliance for Economic Democracy had been offered posts in the new government. They all were extremely busy at this time.

One night after dinner, I lay in bed with my hands clasped behind my head thinking of all that had transpired over the past weeks. I had laid to rest the ghosts of my past, but was it possible to still regain my wife and family? Would she, could she, trust me again? Had too much damage been done? I had to find all this out. So I got out of bed, dressed, and headed over to the pay phone in nearby Redman's Shopping Plaza.

'Are you sure you still want to rent the house?' Simone asked.

'Everything's set for it.'

'You don't have much time.'

'I know. I'm looking forward to coming home.'

'Home?'

187

'You were right all along,' I said. 'I needed to come here. I needed to face up to some things here. I'm all right now.'

I hesitated. If I decided to return to the States, I had to know, emotionally, what I was returning to. I had to know if there was any hope of getting my family back. All I heard was the receiver popping with static.

'Hello...hello....'

'I'm still here,' Simone said.

'But what about us?' I finally blurted out. 'What about us? Do you... can you still love me?'

'There'll always be a part of me that loves you, Alphonso. But me and the girls need to be on our own right now. I don't want to send them through any more changes. They've been through enough already.' Simone paused and then added, 'Friends?'

'Friends,' I said. 'But we have to talk more when I'm back. Take care of yourself, Simone. And give the girls a hug for me.'

I left the Plaza and drove slowly home. I could not in all honesty have expected a different response, but I felt crushed. I would have to prove to Simone that I'd changed my ways. My thoughts turned to the house. Should I sell instead of rent, after all? Or should I pay someone to maintain it and use it as a vacation home? By the time I reached home, I'd concluded that selling the house would probably be the best thing to do. Christopher would handle the sale. I could have the rental agreement cancelled. I would return to the States. To Wesslar. To my daughters.

Next morning, I headed to Mrs. Lashley's to call Christopher about my change of plan. As I walked down the road, I gazed over the landscape that had fashioned me. I passed the empty house lot with its rotting tree stump. The faint odour of cow dung reached me, and a brown and white cow, chewing its cud next to the stump, gazed dreamily at me, its tail sluggishly whipping flies off its backside. Everywhere else around the houses was a shock of green, testament to the recent rains. I looked above at the blue eggshell-crisp sky adorned with woolly cirrus clouds and felt a renewed affinity with this place so deep that it was painful. I stopped in the middle of the road and looked back at the house I had just left. For a moment, I imagined the spot empty save for the oleanders, Pride of Barbados, crotons, and other trees. It was a disturbing sight. Something important was gone. It seemed as if something crucial in me, a rediscovered root, would be lost again, this time forever. The thought that the house was all I had left of my Barbadian family pierced me like a nail. I knew I had to keep it. I couldn't sell. I just couldn't.

I started walking back toward GOOD HOPE knowing my family spirits were all at rest but also knowing that I couldn't physically stay in the island. I would leave in a few days. Christopher and Phyllis would be disappointed, I knew. He had been offered the post of Leader of the House and had accepted the position. But he would keep his property management business going. Over lunch, he told me that if I remained in the island, a job with the government's engineering projects would be mine. That thought warmed and reassured me, but the need to be near my daughters was greater. I reached the house and entered through the front door. With someone living in it, GOOD HOPE would be maintained, would be kept from disintegrating as my family had done over the years. The house embodied my departed. In this light, it held me to them; held me to myself.

ABOUT THE AUTHOR

Anthony Kellman was born in Barbados in 1955, educated at Combermere School, at UWI (Cave Hill) and in the U.S. At eighteen he left for Britain where he worked as a troubadour playing pop and West Indian folk music on the pub and folk club circuit. During the 1980s he returned to Barbados where he worked as a newspaper reporter, then did a BA in English and History. Afterwards he worked in PR for the Central Bank of Barbados, experiences which he drew on in writing *The Coral Rooms*.

At this time he published two poetry chapbooks, *In Depths of Burning Lights* (1982) and *The Broken Sun* (1984), which drew praise from Kamau Brathwaite, among others.

In 1987 he left Barbados for the USA where he studied for a Masters of Fine Arts degree in Creative Writing at Lousiana State University. After completing in 1989 he moved to Augusta State University, Georgia, where he is a professor of English and creative writing.

In 1990 Peepal Tree published his third book of poetry, *Watercourse*, (which appeared with a glowing endorsement from Edouard Glissant), the novel, *The Coral Rooms* (1994), *The Long Gap* (1996) and *Wings of a Stranger* (2000). All his work has a powerful involvement with landscape, both as a living entity shaping peoples' lives and as a source of metaphor for inner processes. The limestone caves of Barbados have provided a particularly fertile source of inspiration.

He is currently working on a long narrative poem written in the rhythms of tuk, the indigenous musical form of Barbados. In 1992 he edited the first full-length U.S. anthology of English-speaking Caribbean poetry, *Crossing Water*. A recipient of a National Endowment for the Arts fellowship, his poetry, fiction and critical essays have appeared in journals all over the world.

ALSO BY ANTHONY KELLMAN

The Coral Rooms
0 948833 53 X   102pp   £6.95

Percival Veer has risen to the tenth floor of the Federal Bank of Charouga, has acquired a large and imposing house and a young and attentive wife. But satisfaction eludes him. Guilt over a past wrong begins to trouble him and a recurrent dream of caves disturbs his sleep. As Percy's inner world crumbles, he is gripped by an obsessive desire to explore the deep limestone caves of his island, dimly remembered from his boyhood. This gripping, poetic novel charts Percy's meeting with his spiritual guide, Cane Arrow, and his hallucinatory descent into the cave's depths.

Percival Veer's journey through the caves is not only a journey to truths that lie within him, but a journey to a vision of 'Creole magic': 'worlds of possibilities, coalescing visions and revisions of races and their juxtapositions.' This vision contrasts sharply with the cynical and pragmatic world of ethnic politics which has been his corrupting environment as a career bureaucrat.

'Realistic and dreamlike, explicit and mysterious... The descriptions are evocative & sensual. A compelling read.'
- Carole Klein.

'A realistic and convincing portrait of self-loathing'
- Wilson Harris.

Watercourse
0 948833 37 8   64pp   £5.99

The celebrated Martiniquan poet and novelist Edouard Glissant writes: '*Watercourse* is more than a collection of poems. It is the continual amazement evoked by Caribbean landscape: a single dialogue between the sea and the land... a song whose dazzling waves foam among the islands... Anthony Kellman's poetry has the strength and sweetness of vegetation with the power of progressively revealing to us the nature of the earth in which it grows.'

Joseph Bruchac writes: 'His enchantment is that dangerous, double-edged power of a Prospero, a magician who has visioned life in all its complexity...'

The Long Gap
0 948833 78 5   64pp   £6.99

The Long Gap is a passionate exploration of the Caribbean exile's need 'to go back/to clutch the roots of the word'. Writing out of the the fear of the 'gap' which can grow too long, Kellman engages with his Barbadian heritage as one which both sustains and drives to anger. In language which echoes the rhythms of the 'tuk' band and the 'scat of the guitar strum', he celebrates the traditions of resistance and creative invention, but excoriates the islands of cocaine, political corruption and subservience to external masters.

Bruce King writes: 'Tony Kellman is always trying something different... He is a serious poet and the various contradictions and affiliations found in his verse embody those of the Caribbean and, to generalise, most poetry. A formalist attracted towards, oral, folk and popular traditions, he also mixes the highly lyrical with dialect and the prose-like. I especially like his metaphors and patterns of sound. When reading these poems you feel that... here is one of our best younger poets.'

Wings of a Stranger
1 900715 44 9   71pp   £7.99

In the continuing rite of return to his native Barbados from longer and longer away, something has happened for Tony Kellman. No longer are these the alienated poems of *the long gap*, of belonging nowhere. With greater establishment in America has come, *on the wings of a stranger*, the capacity to embrace this past and to see wholly afresh what was once familiar and unremarked. Parallel to these poems of place, are those that explore new love and its power to heal.

As well as Barbados, there are poems set in worlds as different as sharecropping Georgia and Yorkshire, England. In all of them one hears Kellman's signal voice which combines his urbane capacity to 'hum forever simple pleasure' and the ecstatic vision of a poet who 'puts on the garment of praise' to 'retell our special story'.

All these books and over 140 other Caribbean, Black British and South Asian titles can be bought on Peepal Tree's website on a secure server: www.peepaltreepress.com or by mail order from: Peepal Tree Press, 17 King's Avenue, Leeds LS6 1QS Telephone: (+44) 0113 245 1703 2 Email: hannah@peepaltreepress.com